BONE-BREAKIN' BULLY

"Kill the bastard! Rip his head clean off, Mr. Beck!"

Elias sleeved blood from his lips and turned around to face Shiloh.

"Elias," Shiloh said, "you sure are slow to learn your manners around me."

Shiloh tried to jump back but wasn't able to escape the big man's outstretched arms. Elias caught him in a bear hug and then slammed Shiloh with his forehead, trying to break his nose.

Shiloh could hardly breathe, the man was so strong. He knew he had to break free or he'd be crushed....

* * *

SPECIAL PREVIEW!

Turn to the back of this book for a sneak-peek excerpt from the exciting, brand-new Western series...

FURY

... **the blazing story of a gunfighting legend.**

Books in the SHILOH series by Dalton Walker

SHILOH
SHILOH 2: DESERT HELL
SHILOH 3: BLOOD RIVAL
SHILOH 4: THE HUNTED
SHILOH 5: HELL TOWN
SHILOH 6: SIDEWINDER
SHILOH 7: VENGEANCE TRAIL
SHILOH 8: BLOOD BOUNTY

SHILOH

BLOOD BOUNTY

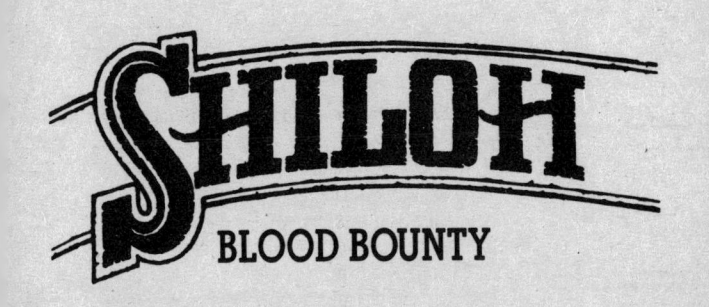

DALTON WALKER

DIAMOND BOOKS, NEW YORK

BLOOD BOUNTY

A Diamond Book / published by arrangement with
the author

PRINTING HISTORY
Diamond edition / July 1992

All rights reserved.
Copyright © 1992 by Charter Communications, Inc.
Material excerpted from *Fury* by Jim Austin
copyright © 1992 by The Berkley Publishing Group.
This book may not be reproduced in whole or
in part, by mimeograph or any other means, without
permission. For information address:
The Berkley Publishing Group,
200 Madison Avenue, New York, New York 10016.

ISBN: 1-55773-744-4

Diamond Books are published by The Berkley Publishing Group,
200 Madison Avenue, New York, New York 10016.
The name "DIAMOND" and its logo are trademarks
belonging to Charter Communications, Inc.

PRINTED IN THE UNITED STATES OF AMERICA

10 9 8 7 6 5 4 3 2 1

SHILOH
BLOOD BOUNTY

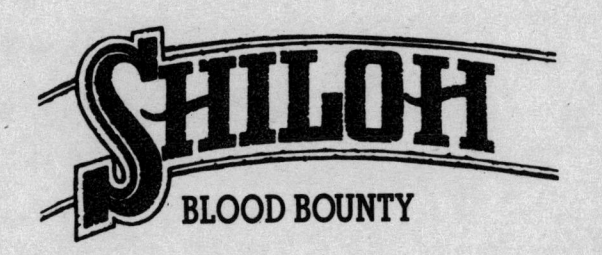

1

SHILOH WAS IN no particular hurry and he had no particular place to go except to find and kill Harry Dawson. Well, it wasn't certain that he'd kill Dawson, because the Wanted poster that Shiloh carried wadded up in his hip pocket said dead or alive. Thing of it was, though, Harry Dawson had always said that no man would ever take him back to prison. The deadly outlaw had vowed that he would rather fight to the death.

That was fine with Shiloh. Dawson's reward poster made it clear that the man had killed more than ten innocent men, if you didn't count Indians, Chinamen and Mexicans. If you counted them, Dawson had probably killed more than two dozen.

It was a cold spring day and Shiloh was tired of his nose running as he rode into the teeth of a hard Wyoming wind. The only good thing Shiloh could think about was how he'd find a warm saloon, a hot bath and maybe an even hotter woman in the ranching town of Elk, less than a mile up ahead. Shiloh had been through Elk a time or two and he'd always found it hospitable enough. There were four saloons, a couple of pretty good places to eat and one of the best whorehouses in the territory. A man with money could find a poker game or a woman just about as easy as he could blow his damned nose.

When Shiloh rode into Elk a short time later he saw that very little had changed. The same businesses still existed, and it didn't appear that the town had either grown or diminished in size. His first stop was the livery, where he dismounted and hoped to step out of the wind.

"Hey, Walt!" he called, leading his horse up to the big livery barn doors. "You in there?"

Walt Hostettler came hobbling out. He wasn't an old man, probably no more than forty-five, but he had lived hard. In his younger days he'd been a mustanger and a bronc buster, and by the age of thirty he'd had all his ribs and limbs broken and had lost track of how many times his skull had been fractured. Now, his face was set in a grimace and Shiloh knew the man moved with constant pain.

"How you doin', old man?" Shiloh said, thumbing back his dirty Stetson and grinning.

Walt spat a stream of tobacco between Shiloh's boots. "I'm doin' just fine. Not gettin' rich, but then you just arrived."

"Ha!" Shiloh reached into his pockets and pulled them inside out. "No money this time."

"Then get the hell outa here," Walt said, turning away. "This ain't no charity I'm runnin'."

"But my horse is half starved and goin' lame," Shiloh protested, leading the animal after the man into the dim interior of the barn. "Which stall?"

"Third one down on the right," Walt barked as he found an empty horseshoe keg and eased his weight off his feet. "Who the hell are you bound and determined to kill this time?"

"Harry Dawson. You see him in town lately?"

"Last month he and a couple of his men spent the night at Darla's Place. She kicked him out about six in the morning. I hear he just tormented the bejesus out of her girls. Darla says that she'll never let Harry or his boys back in her place."

"Well, that will cause her some trouble," Shiloh said. "Could be Darla might be willing to give me a little free service if I promise to kill or bring Harry to justice."

"You're always thinking of an angle, ain't you, Shiloh."

"A man hasn't got much choice in these times," Shiloh said. "Money is harder to come by than ever before. Hell, Walt, I'm bringing in bank robbers for bounties that I'd have laughed at a few years back."

"Why is that? Banks and trains carrying less money to rob?"

Shiloh shrugged. He was lean with wolf-gray eyes and broad shoulders. He was of average height but was thick in the chest and upper arms so that he was imposing in his blue Union pants and torn coat, wore black boots and an Army Colt on his hip. Anyone who saw him knew at first glance that Shiloh was neither a cowboy, a miner nor a gambler. What he was was a man that needed to be walked around when he looked to be in a foul mood.

Pulling his saddle off and dropping it over a saddle rack, Shiloh complained, "There's just too damn much competition these days in my business. Used to be all I had to worry about was the Pinkerton agents. Now, every two-bit gunnie thinks he can be a bounty hunter. Most of them get shot, of course, before they collect a dime."

"Of course," Walt said. "How many times have you been shot?"

"Lost track," Shiloh said, leading his horse into the stall and then removing its bridle before stepping out and locking the stall door. "Maybe six or seven times. Every one of them by ambush."

"You mean to tell me you've never been beaten in a stand-up gunfight?"

"Not yet," Shiloh said. "There are faster men but none I've faced as steady. Gettin' a gun out first is only half the battle for a greenhorn shooter. Hitting what you aim for without a miss is what counts."

"I suppose," Walt said. "They tell me that Harry Dawson is just another damn back-shooter."

"He's a little more than that," Shiloh said. "Dawson will ambush a man, and he rarely faces anyone in a stand-up gunfight unless he's cornered. But to me, that just shows that he's a smart man. Only a fool gives his enemy a chance of gunning him down."

At this Walt snorted, "Hell, Shiloh! You're not much better than Harry if you believe that."

"Sure I am," Shiloh argued. "I've never ambushed anyone and I never shot anyone in the back. And finally, I don't run with a pack of dogs that kill for sport."

"So how much will you collect if you kill Dawson before he kills you?" the liveryman asked.

"Two hundred dollars."

Walt snorted in derision. "Hell, that ain't hardly worth the risk! Not considering you have to take on Harry Dawson's men in order to kill him."

"That's right," Shiloh said. "But at least his boys are also wanted. An extra hundred or two will come in handy."

"If you live to collect it," Walt said. "I've been around these parts long enough to have figured out that Harry Dawson isn't a man to be taken lightly. He's a mean, cunning bastard, and the men he rides with are of the same cut."

BLOOD BOUNTY

"Goes with the job," Shiloh said. He reached into his coat pocket and dragged out a few dollars. "Here. This is in advance."

Walt took the money. "With someone in your line of work, I always appreciate being paid in advance, Shiloh."

"I understand." Shiloh turned to leave. "This town still bought and paid for by Cephas Beck?"

"Not my stable!"

"Well," Shiloh said at the door, "maybe not your place, but about every other one in Elk."

Walt scowled. "It galls a man the way the Becks parade around here like they not only own the biggest cattle ranch in this part of Wyoming, but that they also think they're about ten notches better than any other man."

"You could sell out to Cephas," Shiloh said. "I know he's made you some pretty good offers over the past few years."

"If I did that, I'd have trouble looking at myself in the mirror," Walt said. "You know I worked for old Cephas almost ten years. The last time a bronc fell on me and broke my leg in three places, Cephas just watched them carry me to the bunkhouse. Next day he came in and paid me my wages and told me to pull my freight. He said he couldn't use a bronc buster who wasn't able to ride."

"He's a damned hard man all right," Shiloh said. "Is that son of his still terrorizing the town?"

"You mean Elias?"

"That's the only son that Cephas has got, isn't it?"

"Yeah, thank God! That big bastard is even meaner than his pa. He broke a bottle across a dancehall girl's face last week. She wasn't pretty to begin with, but when that glass shattered . . . well, let's just say that the only way you'd want her now would be in the dark."

Shiloh frowned. "I hate to hear about such a thing as that. Elias is too damn big and strong to be whippin' a woman with a bottle. Anyone try to stop him from cutting her like that?"

Walt looked at him like he was crazy, and that caused Shiloh to just shake his head and turn away. He didn't have to ask why no one tried to help the woman, because he knew that everyone in this town was either beholden to Cephas Beck or afraid of him and his half-crazed, ox-sized son.

"You watch out for Elias!" Walt shouted. "He hasn't forgotten the last time you were through here and got the drop on him. You shouldn't have made him beg for his life."

"He needed a lesson in humility," Shiloh replied as he headed out for the saloon and a bottle of whiskey. "And there just didn't seem to be anyone else in this town that was man enough to administer the lesson except me."

"Can I have your horse and saddle when either Elias pounds your brains out or Dawson shoots you in the back!"

Shiloh did not dignify the question with a reply. He had not come to Elk, Wyoming, to either get his brains beat out or shot from ambush. What brought him here was the fact that this was the most likely jumping-off point to find Dawson's trail. Once that was accomplished, he could track the outlaw and his band down and then figure out how to kill them.

What was required in Shiloh's line of work was confidence and ability. A slow or faint-hearted man did not last long in this bloody business. Lose your confidence and you'd quickly lose your life.

2

THE BLUE DOG Saloon was one of Shiloh's favorite Wyoming watering holes. It had a long mahogany bar and a fine back-wall mirror. It boasted gilded pictures of frolicking nymphs and reposing naked maidens. A trophy-size elk's head was mounted just over the back door on the way to the outhouse.

The saloon was doing a good business when Shiloh sauntered in and leaned against the bar. "Hey, Joe, how's your whiskey this month?"

"Same as always."

"That means it'll taste like horse piss and bite like a rabid dog," Shiloh drawled. "Give me half a bottle that some son of a bitch ain't drooled in yet."

"You always was a fussy bastard," Joe said, wiping his hands on a dirty bar rag and moving down to shake with Shiloh. "How you been?"

"Fine," Shiloh replied.

"Who you after this time?"

"Harry Dawson and his boys. You seen them lately?"

" 'Bout two weeks ago they came in for a drink. Stayed a couple of hours. Chased off my regulars and ruined the night's business the same as they always do."

"He pay this time?"

"Hell no!" Joe's face flushed with anger. "He always says, 'Put it on my bar tab, Joe.' Then the big bastard laughs like it was a joke. All his boys laugh too. I let 'em each take a bottle and they leave without shooting up the place."

"I mean to put a stop to that," Shiloh said. "I think Dawson and his boys have been pushing folks like you around way too long. They robbed another bank over in Dry Creek last month. Shot the bank manager down in cold blood."

"Why the hell don't some U.S. marshal deputize a bunch of men and go after Dawson?"

"Why?" Shiloh asked, removing the cork from the bottle of whiskey Joe had handed him and taking a long pull. "The reason is that one U.S. marshal did go after Dawson, and neither he nor the six men he deputized have been seen since."

"And so you're going to do what seven men could not?" Joe asked skeptically.

"Yes, sir," Shiloh said. "My thinking is that once I kill Dawson, the others won't be that hard to arrest. Dawson is the man with all the brains and guts. A man like that doesn't choose to ride with equals. You'll always find him surrounded by followers. Take away their leader and they lose the will to fight."

Joe scoffed. "Hell, whatever you say, Shiloh! You choose to believe that, it's your funeral, not mine. I'd think Elias Beck would be plenty enough for you to worry about in Elk. He finds out you're in town, he'll come looking for you."

"Tell him I'm easy to find," Shiloh said, taking another pull on his bottle of whiskey.

"Ain't no bounty on Elias," Joe said. "I'd think since there was no money to be made, you might just try and be a little more sociable to Elias."

Shiloh snorted in derision. "When a man starts to cozy up to a rattlesnake, he shouldn't be surprised when he gets bit. Elias is a bully and a fool. He'll keep pushing folks around until someone kills him."

"Someone like you?"

"Maybe. Depends on him. I'm willing to let bygones be bygones."

"Hell yes you are! You got the drop on him and made him beg for his life. To a man like Elias, that was a terrible thing, Shiloh."

"He deserved it. I hear he used a bottle on a woman last week. Hear he messed her face up pretty bad."

"Something awful," Joe said. "She hasn't come out of her room yet. She let it be known that she'll take men at night, but no one is interested in making love to a woman with a broken face—even if you can't see it."

"What's her name?"

"Josey. I don't know what will become of her."

"The same thing that becomes of all whores," Shiloh said quietly. "They get disease or they get killed by some drunken bully like Elias. Never seen one that didn't come to a sad end. Maybe this will save her life by forcing her to find another line of work."

"Who would hire an ex-whore whose face was all beat up and scarred?"

"I don't know," Shiloh snapped, not wanting to think about it. "But I've never seen anyone starve who was willing to take any kind of honest work."

"You got a good point there," Joe said, moving away to serve another customer.

For the next hour, Shiloh relaxed at the bar, talking to a few of the customers whose faces he recognized. He made it a point to ask each one if they'd seen Harry Dawson, but no one had seen him in several weeks.

"He's probably in Colorado," one man surmised. "Or maybe down in the Utah country raisin' hell with old

Brigham Young and his Mormons."

"Could be he's clear over in Nevada," another man said. "I heard he killed a man on the Comstock Lode last year. Some of his men were from over in that part of the country."

Shiloh just listened and nodded his head without making comment. It was always this way when you first started trying to get a lead on a wanted man. You heard everyone giving you an opinion about things they didn't know. If he followed every rumor, a bounty hunter would run himself to death, if he didn't starve first.

It was late in the afternoon when Shiloh decided he was getting hungry enough to wolf down a steak dinner after a hot bath and a shave. He sauntered over to the Outland Hotel and paid for a week's lodging.

"Good to have you stay with us, Mr. Shiloh," the hotel desk clerk said with a nervous smile.

"You new on the job?" Shiloh asked, sizing up the thin, asthenic man.

"Yes, sir."

"Then how come you know my name?"

"Well, sir, I've heard a lot about you. I sure hope you and Mr. Elias Beck have settled your differences."

"Why?"

The clerk swallowed noisily. "Well, sir. It's just that we don't allow any shooting in the rooms. You can understand that, can't you?"

"Of course. Blood is hard to get out of the rugs," Shiloh deadpanned.

The clerk paled, then stammered, "Well, sir . . . I . . . I mean that's not what I meant!"

"Don't worry," Shiloh said, taking his key and heading for the staircase. "All you have to do is keep Elias from coming up these stairs to try and kill me."

"But . . . but how can I do that! His father *owns* this hotel."

Shiloh paused, one foot poised on the stairs. "Well, then, if I have to kill that big fool Elias, your rug cleaning bill will just have to come out of Cephas Beck's profits the same as his son's burial."

Shiloh saw the clerk's jaw drop and then he turned and went on up to his room, calling, "Don't forget to send up that hot water for my bath!"

That evening, freshly scrubbed and shaved, Shiloh had a pretty decent steak at the Mother Lode Café, which was also owned by Cephas Beck.

"I suppose old Cephas even supplies the beefsteak you fed me," Shiloh said, wiping the grease from his lips with a napkin.

"Yes, sir," the café owner said, anxiously glancing at the door. "But to tell you the truth, I ain't so sure that Elias and some of the Circle Bar riders won't be comin' in here this evening for a steak. I'd sort of be grateful if you paid up and didn't hang around any."

"You trying to get rid of me?" Shiloh asked, feigning surprise.

"Well, not exactly, sir. But I just don't want any trouble, and I ain't sure that it's all that healthy for you to hang around these parts. Elias has been mustanging all week, and this bein' Friday he just might want to storm into town and go on a tear."

"Well," Shiloh drawled, "it's his father's town, no reason he shouldn't be allowed to raise hell."

"Yeah, but . . . well, sir, I'd prefer that he didn't do it in here."

Shiloh stood up. There was just enough perversity in him to want to stay and watch this man sweat, but, on the other hand, he thought he'd enjoy sitting in on a game of poker over at the Blue Dog Saloon for a few hours before he went to bed.

"You seen or heard anything of Harry Dawson and his boys?" Shiloh asked, paying his bill.

"Well, sir, actually I have! I heard he was down in Santa Fe, New Mexico. Heard that's where he was these days. I'm sure you could find him if you went right down there and started looking."

Shiloh shook his head. "Santa Fe is a long ways off. If I had to ride that far, I might decide it'd be easier to find another wanted man to hunt down for the bounty. Ought to be any number of them closer to Elk than that."

"Well, sir, there's probably a lot of money on Dawson's head. I think it'd be worth your time to go to Santa Fe. I sure enough do."

"Thanks for the advice," Shiloh growled, heading for the door.

"And if Elias Beck does come in for a steak, say hello for me. Tell him I'll be playin' poker over at the Blue Dog and he might just want to come and join me for a little fun."

"Yes, sir!"

Shiloh walked back out into the street chuckling to himself. It was amazing how worried everyone was about his health if he met up with Elias Beck. The truth of it was, they would be better off to worry about Elias's health.

3

SHILOH WAS ALMOST ready to cash in his chips and call it a night at the Blue Dog when big Elias Beck slammed through the batwing doors. The room fell silent, and Shiloh eased his chair back from the table so that, if necessary, he could made a clean play for his six-gun. When three other men filtered into the saloon to flank Elias, the poker players departed so hastily that they didn't even bother to scoop up their chips. Shiloh was more than happy to do that for them. He guessed that earned him another thirty dollars at least.

"Well, well!" Elias boomed. "Look what the cat dragged in!"

Shiloh stuffed the chips into his coat pocket and walked over to the bar, where Joe was standing looking very worried. "I'd like to cash these in," Shiloh said. "Think I'll call it a night just like the boys at our table."

"For Chrissakes!" Joe hissed. "Forget the chips! Get out the back door!"

Shiloh ignored the advice. He could see Elias out of the corner of his eyes, and the big man had not moved from the doorway. "Cash 'em in, Joe," Shiloh ordered in a calm voice. "I won't leave without my winnings."

"You won't leave standing!"

"Cash 'em, Joe."

Joe frantically cashed in the chips. "There!" he cried.

"Forty-four dollars. Now why don't you . . ."

"Thanks," Shiloh growled, scooping up the money and shoving it into his coat before he turned and faced Elias Beck and his three friends. The three men did not greatly concern Shiloh because he could tell at a glance that they weren't gunmen. They looked like mustangers or bronc busters, and he recalled that Elias had been mustanging all week.

"You boys look tired and thirsty," Shiloh said. "Mustanging is hard, dangerous work. I'd be happy to buy you a drink."

Elias came forward and stopped just a few feet from Shiloh. "I'll take that drink, bounty hunter."

"Joe," Shiloh called, tossing a couple of dollars on the bar, "pour Elias and his friends some whiskey. Leave the bottle."

Joe poured but was so nervous that the neck of the whiskey bottle chattered against the rim of the glasses, causing him to spill as much as he managed to get into the glasses.

"Let's just all settle down and be friends, eh, Elias? There's no sense in stirring up old troubles. What is done is done and . . ."

"Shut up!"

Joe shut up fast. He gulped and moved off down the bar while Shiloh reached for a glass and poured himself a shot. "Any luck mustanging?" he asked with an easy smile.

"Yeah, we caught the finest stallion in Wyoming just this morning. And now, I come in to celebrate and find you. This must be my lucky day."

"Keep it lucky," Shiloh warned softly. "Just drink your whiskey and behave yourself."

"And if I don't?"

"Then I'm afraid that I'll just have to give you another lesson in humility," Shiloh said without a trace of hostility. "But I'd hoped that you'd learned your lesson for keeps after the last time."

Elias paled. He was a good four inches taller than Shiloh and fifty pounds of muscle heavier. He had hands as big as hams and his square, meaty face was burned raw by the sun. His nose was busted and his eyes were deep-set and black. Right now, they were gleaming with pure hatred.

"Be a good boy," Shiloh told the man in a voice too low to be heard by anyone except Elias, "or I'll humiliate you again."

Something snapped in Elias Beck. Shiloh saw it and he hurled his whiskey, glass and all, into Elias's face. The man cried out in fury and Shiloh filled the open mouth with a row of hard knuckles.

Elias backpedaled rapidly and probably would have gone down except that his men caught and supported him until he could clear his eyes of whiskey.

"I'm gonna tear your arms and legs off!" Elias bellowed.

Shiloh looked to the other three men. "You got enough help," he taunted.

Elias whirled on his men. His lips were smears of blood and he spat, "You boys stay the hell out of it, understand! This is between him and me!"

The mustangers nodded grimly. One hissed, "Kill the bastard! Rip his head clean off, Mr. Beck!"

Elias sleeved blood from his lips and turned around to face Shiloh, who had not moved one inch. The bounty hunter's hand was hanging near the butt of his six-gun and he looked perfectly relaxed and totally confident, just as he intended.

"Elias," Shiloh said, "you sure are slow to learn your manners around me."

Elias roared and came charging forward. Shiloh ducked a ponderous overhead right and drove his own fist into Elias's belly. It was like striking the face of a Cheyenne war drum and his fist bounced off. You could say that Elias wasn't bright and you'd be correct, but you could not say that he wasn't solid muscle.

Elias crashed into the bar and wheeled around, but not before Shiloh stepped in and pounded him in both kidneys.

"Ugggh!" Elias grunted twice as he staggered around to be greeted by Shiloh's fist as it exploded against his jaw.

Elias staggered, caught himself on the bar and lurched forward. Shiloh tried to jump back but wasn't able to escape the big man's outstretched arms. Elias caught him in a bear hug and then slammed Shiloh with his forehead, trying to break his nose.

Shiloh just managed to turn his head and Elias's forehead connected solidly with his ear. It hurt like the blazes, and Shiloh retaliated by driving the heel of his boot down Elias's shinbone.

"Owww!" the man cried as Shiloh did it again on the other leg. "Owww!"

Shiloh tried to break free but Elias would not let him go. Again, the big man slammed at Shiloh with his forehead, and it caused his ears to ring and the left side of his face to go numb. Furthermore, Elias was threatening to cave in Shiloh's ribs. Shiloh could hardly breathe the man was so strong, and he knew he had to break free or be crushed.

He drove both of his thumbs into Elias's nostrils right up to the first joint, and the man bellowed in pain as

Shiloh forced his head back to expose his thick throat. Shiloh yanked his right thumb free, drew back his fist and hammered Elias in his Adam's apple.

The big rancher's eyes bugged and he struggled to hang on to Shiloh, but he couldn't breathe very well, and when Shiloh punched him in the throat again and tried to rip his nostril open, Elias had no choice but to release his bear hug.

Shiloh drew a deep breath and drew back his fist. Timing his punch and putting every ounce of his weight behind it, he drove his fist into the side of Elias's jaw. The man's eyes rolled up in his head. He made a feeble effort to hang on to the lip of the bar, but his legs buckled and he dropped to his knees. Shiloh, ears ringing and gasping for breath, stepped back and kneed the man full in the face. The back of Elias's head cracked against the bar and he pitched forward. When he struck the floor, he didn't even quiver.

Shiloh lurched backward, hand reaching for his pistol as the three Circle Bar mustangers charged him. Had Shiloh been clear headed and fresh, he'd have cleared leather and gunned down all three, but they overpowered him and drove him to the floor, then began to stomp and kick him.

Shiloh tried to cover his head and turn his back to them. If he could get to his feet with his gun in his fist, he knew he'd kill them for certain. But they must have known that too because they were on him like a pack of winter-starved wolves and they didn't let up on him an instant until he was flat on his belly getting the life stomped out of him.

Dimly, he heard the roar of a shotgun and Joe's voice warning the three Circle Bar men to back off or he'd blow them to hell. They must have believed Joe because the blows stopped falling on Shiloh. A moment later, he drifted into a dark tunnel and lost consciousness.

"All right," Joe said, "you boys get Elias out of here. Get a wagon and take him back to the ranch."

"You're making a real bad mistake, Joe," one of the cowboys said. "A real stupid mistake backing that man over Elias."

"I ain't backin' anyone!" Joe said. "I'm just preventing a murder. You tell Mr. Beck I said that. You tell him I knew he wouldn't want you to murder a helpless man."

"Mr. Beck will see you pay for this," the cowboy promised. "He'll say we should have stomped Shiloh to death and been done with him for good."

"Get Elias out of here," Joe said, the shotgun steady in his hands. "You tell Mr. Beck that I won't be allowing Shiloh back into the Blue Dog Saloon ever again."

"You're finished in Elk," a second cowboy grated. "Mr. Beck will shoot you himself."

Joe figured that the man was right. He had operated Cephas Beck's saloon for eight years and he knew how hard and uncompromising the old rancher could be. Cephas would view this action as a betrayal and he'd come riding into Elk to seek revenge.

"Git!" Joe shouted.

"You're a dead man, Joe. You just don't realize it yet."

Joe said nothing until the Circle Bar mustangers had hauled Elias out of the Blue Dog Saloon. Then he placed his shotgun on the bar and untied his white apron.

One of the patrons asked, "What are you going to do now, Joe?"

"I'm leaving Elk for good."

"Well . . . well what about him!"

Joe looked down at Shiloh. "Hell," he sighed, "I've

lost my job to save his life and that was a damn fool thing to do. Reckon it'd be even more foolish to have it all go for naught. Help me get him up and in a chair."

They dragged Shiloh upright and got him in a chair. He was still unconscious, but when Joe pried open his mouth and jammed a bottle of whiskey between his teeth, then grabbed his hair and bent his head back to pour, Shiloh choked and regained his senses.

"Shiloh? Shiloh, listen to me," Joe said. "I'm leaving Elk within the hour. If you want to come along, I'll help you to your horse and we can ride off together. If Cephas Beck and his men come after me, it'd be good to have a man like you riding by my side. You want to come with me?"

"No," Shiloh gasped, feeling the whiskey burn his gullet.

"Man, do you realize what the hell you are sayin'! If you stay here, Cephas is sure to come to kill you! Your only hope is to ride out with me."

Shiloh raised his head a little. "I'm staying," he wheezed.

"But . . ."

"Thanks, Joe. Now get me to my bed and ride out if you've a mind to."

Joe shook his head. "You look awful. Them Circle Bar boys just kicked you nearly to death. I guess they kicked the sense right out of your head."

Joe looked at one of the men. "I need some help to get him over to his hotel room. Anybody willing?"

They all backed away, and one of the men said, "We heard what was said about Mr. Beck coming to kill you 'cause you helped Shiloh. Don't reckon any of us want to help bad enough to make Mr. Beck kill us. You can understand that, can't you, Joe?"

The bartender nodded and managed to get Shiloh to stand. "Sure I can. Shiloh and I are big enough fools to go around without adding any of you fellas."

Then Joe helped Shiloh outside. The cold evening air cleared the bounty hunter's senses and revived him a little.

"I sure can't thank you enough," Shiloh mumbled. "I was a goner until you fired that shotgun."

"You're a goner anyway if you stay in Elk and wait for Cephas to come and pay you back for whipping his son again."

"Maybe, maybe not. It was a fair fight between just the two of us until them other sonsabitches jumped on me."

"I wish you'd change your mind and ride out with me," Joe said.

"Can't."

"Why not?"

" 'Cause I've already paid a week's room rent at this hotel," Shiloh said.

Joe cursed and helped Shiloh into the hotel. The minute the desk clerk saw Shiloh's bloody face he came scooting around his counter.

"You can't bring that man in here in this condition!"

"Try and stop me," Joe hissed. "Just try, Herb."

"Was it Elias did this to him? Did he fight Elias again?"

"Yep, and Shiloh whipped his ass. Only thing is, some of the Circle Bar men got to him hard."

Herb groaned. "Oh, man! You can't bring him in here! Mr. Beck *owns* this hotel. If he finds Shiloh here, he might think I helped him."

"So join the crowd," Joe snarled, pushing past the man and taking Shiloh upstairs.

"Which room!"

"Number 214, but . . ."

Joe didn't wait to hear the rest. He took Shiloh up, and when he discovered that the door was locked, rather than trouble Shiloh for his room key he kicked open the door then dragged Shiloh across the room to his bed.

"Shiloh?"

"Huh?"

"It'll take me a good hour or two before I can get all my things packed and my horse saddled. Are you sure you don't want to come along?"

"I'm sure. But thanks, Joe." Shiloh found that he was having a little trouble breathing. His chest felt as if it had been crushed, and maybe it had.

"Damn," Joe said. "You are the most stubborn man I ever seen."

"Get out of town, Joe," Shiloh whispered.

"You can't stay here," Joe said. "Cephas will come and shoot you in bed."

"Then I won't be here."

"Well, then why won't you come with me?"

In answer, Shiloh raised his hand. "Thanks again. And good luck. If we ever cross paths again, I owe you a big favor."

"We won't cross paths unless it's in hell," Joe said, turning to leave. "And unless we both get lucky, that might not be very long from now."

When the door closed, Shiloh pushed himself to his feet and staggered over to throw a dead bolt in place. Next, he managed to reach his nightstand, and over it was a mirror. Only when Shiloh saw his reflection did he fully realize how savage a beating he'd taken in the Blue Dog Saloon.

"I'll remember them damn mustangers," he mumbled

between swollen lips. "And if I can get through this business with Cephas, I'll settle the score with all three."

Shiloh bent and cupped water in his hands, then doused his bloody face. He doused it again and again, trying to clear his mind. He probably had been crazy to decline Joe's offer, but running wasn't his nature. Besides, Elias had been the one to provoke the fight—Shiloh figured all he'd really done was finish it.

He removed his bloodstained shirt and used it to towel his face dry. It was bruised and battered but it would heal. What he needed to do now was to think a little about his next course of action.

Shiloh staggered over to his bed and found his jacket and the makings. He rolled a cigarette, and when it was lit he inhaled greedily. The tobacco settled his nerves and he felt better. He needed a clearer head and a little time to think. Cephas Beck, he was sure, would not arrive for a day or two.

By then, Shiloh thought, stretching out on the bed and closing his eyes, I will either be gone or I'll be ready to fight.

4

LATE THAT NIGHT, Shiloh was awakened by a pounding that he at first thought was in his head. Only after it grew louder did he open his eyes and sit up, reaching for his Colt even though he was sure that it was too soon to be Cephas or any of his cowboys.

"Who is it?"

There was a long silence. Shiloh cocked back the hammer of his gun, then called again, "Who the hell is it?"

"It's . . . Josey," came a soft voice.

"Josey?" Shiloh whispered. "Who the hell is Josey?"

But even as he asked the question, he remembered that Josey was the whore that Elias had disfigured with a whiskey bottle.

"Hang on," he called, grunting with pain as he pushed to his feet and went to the door. "You alone?"

"Yes. Open up."

Shiloh kept his gun in his fist just in case he was being set up by someone besides the woman. He opened the door a crack and peered into the dim hallway. He saw a woman with a shawl wrapped around her head and the lower half of her face.

"What do you want at this hour?"

"I wanted to thank you for what you did to Elias Beck," she told him. "I wanted to repay you."

"I don't need repaying," Shiloh said. "And I'm sorry about what he did to your face."

Josey stepped past Shiloh into the room. "I thought you might like me tonight since you'll probably be killed tomorrow or the next day."

Shiloh frowned. "Listen, lady, what I need tonight is not a woman, but sleep. I'm pretty banged up, but if I get rest I might be able to think clear enough to decide to leave in the morning."

"You can't! Please don't leave!"

"Well why not?"

"I want you to kill Elias for me!"

Shiloh shook his head. "This crazy talk, woman. I don't kill anyone unless it's for money or in self-defense."

"Then I'll just have to kill Elias myself when he comes for you," she said in a dead voice.

Josey started to leave but Shiloh took her arm and closed the door. "Listen," he told her, "if you try to kill Elias, you'll just end up getting killed yourself. Killing Elias won't make your face right."

"But it will make me feel better," she told him. "Now . . . now the only way that men want me is in the dark. Like this."

She slipped her arms around his neck. "You want me, don't you, Shiloh?"

He swallowed. "My ribs are bruised and my chest hurts every time I take a deep breath. I'm afraid that I couldn't do a thing, Josey. Best if you'd just leave me to sleep."

"Are you sure?" she whispered.

"I'm afraid I am." Shiloh couldn't quite believe what he was saying. The woman's musky scent was driving him crazy, bruised ribs or no bruised ribs.

"All right," she said, sounding very defeated. "But . . . well, I just had to see you. You're the only man I know with the courage to stand up to the Becks."

"Joe Root, the bartender at the Blue Dog Saloon, stood up to them," Shiloh told her. "He risked his life to save mine."

"But then he ran away. I watched him ride out of Elk as if his tail was on fire."

"He's a smart man," Shiloh said.

"I don't care about smart," Josey said, "I care about brave. And I want to stay here with you and fight when they come."

Shiloh gently pushed her back. "Josey, I don't think that would be such a good idea. The last thing I want is for you to be killed on my account."

But Josey wasn't listening. She was feeling. Feeling places that made Shiloh forget all his lofty intentions and encircle the woman in his arms.

"Damn you," he groaned, pushing her down on his bed, "it's been too long since I had a woman."

"How long?" she murmured softly in his ear.

"Two or three weeks at least."

"Then let's take care of that," she said.

Shiloh found he had little choice but to agree. Poor Josey might be a fright in the daylight, but in the soft darkness of his room, she felt beautiful indeed.

She made him forget all about Elias and Cephas Beck.

Elias was conscious by the time he reached the ranch house and dawn was just starting to break over the eastern plains. He had been desperately hoping to die but, since it was increasingly apparent that he would survive this second beating by Shiloh, his next dearest hope was to somehow avoid his father's wrath and contempt.

Now, however, even that modest hope was about to be dashed as old Cephas came hobbling out in his nightshirt to glare at his only son and the returning Circle Bar riders.

"Jeezus kee-rist!" Cephas exploded. "What the hell happened to you this time?"

"Pa, you never mind about it," Elias said, almost tumbling out of his saddle. "I'll take care of him, Pa."

"Take care of *who*?"

"Shiloh."

"He beat you up again!"

Cephas took a menacing step forward. He was still a huge man, though mostly gone to fat. His face was lined and mottled and now it was flushed with anger. His big fists were clenched and his eyes emanated hatred and contempt.

"Now, Pa! You take it easy! 'Member what the doctor said about your heart!"

"The hell with my heart!" Cephas choked. "What's wrong with *your* heart? You big gutless son of a bitch! You let that man whip you twice! If you can't outfight him, you should have gunned him down rather than allow yourself to be humiliated again!"

"We're going to kill him," Elias promised. "He's in town waitin' to see if he can catch Dawson. So just as soon as I'm able, we're going back and gun him down. Make him beg, Pa! He'll beg in front of everyone. You'll see."

Cephas gripped one of the porch posts and his voice shook. "You are one of the most worthless men I've ever had the misfortune to know—much less father!"

The Circle Bar riders looked away feeling embarrassed. This was not the first time they'd seen Elias receive a tongue-lashing and it would probably not be the last. The man was a mean-spirited, lazy and incompetent oaf. The only thing he'd ever done well was fight, and now even that was suspect because of this terrible whipping he'd just received at the hands of Shiloh.

"Pa, you shouldn't ought to talk to me like that," Elias whined, not able to meet his father's eyes. "Especially in front of the men."

"The hell with it!" Cephas bellowed. "They all know you're nothing but an overgrown piece of horseshit! I don't know what the hell to do with you anymore!"

"Well . . . we caught that blue mustang stallion you been wanting for so long! I helped ketch him just as much as the others! And . . . and I mean to break him for you, Pa! I'm good with horses."

"You're good with nothing! If you mess with that stallion he'll finish the job that Shiloh left undone. He'll stomp what few brains you have right into the ground."

"No he won't!" Elias cried out in rage and frustration. "I swear I can break him. You'll see! You'll see!"

"I'll see nothing!" Cephas swung around with an oath on his lips and disappeared into his big ranch house.

For several minutes no one said a word, and then one of the mustangers cleared his throat. "Elias, you'd better let Mike handle that blue stallion. That's why he's getting bronc buster's wages. And with that blue devil, he'll earn every cent of 'em."

"He's right, Elias," another rider said. "That stallion is a killer. You're already beat up enough to—"

With a cry of rage, Elias lashed out with his fist and caught the rider flush on the jaw. The man crashed over backward and Elias booted him in the ribs. The man coiled into a ball, knees to chest, and Elias booted him in the butt. He drew back his foot and would have kicked the rider in the spine except that several of the men grabbed him and pulled him away.

"He didn't mean nothing by that, Elias! Hell, he's one of the ones that put the boots to Shiloh!"

Elias's hair-trigger temper died as quickly as it had flared. "Let go of me," he mumbled, turning away from the writhing figure on the ground as he stumbled toward the ranch house.

"I'm going to ride that blue mustang stallion! You tell Mike that if he even goes near that horse I'll have his hide nailed to our goddamn barn door!"

The Circle Bar riders nodded. "We'll tell him," one said.

Elias looked into the house. He could not see his father and figured the old man had gone back to his room and the fat Mexican woman that he had taken up living with several years ago after his wife had died of fever.

With his blood up and his body in pain, Elias had an overpowering urge to hurt something. Anything. He would have killed the rider still on the ground except that Cephas would have used a bullwhip on his hide.

Elias raised his finger and shook it at the riders. "Tomorrow afternoon. Just before sundown, you have that blue stallion in the breaking corral. You have him snubbed down to the post, saddled and blindfolded. I'm going to ride that blue devil to a standstill or die trying."

The cowboys exchanged glances, and while they clearly thought that Elias's twisted mind had finally snapped, they did not say another word of caution.

"Whatever you say," the foreman said to Elias. "The horse will be ready. If you break him, it'll show a lot of guts, especially considering the shape you're in."

"Nothing wrong with me," Elias hissed. "And you and Pa will see that tomorrow come sundown, when I turn that horse into a damn pussycat as I spur his guts out."

With that, Elias disappeared into the ranch house. After several minutes, one mustanger said, "I hope that big son of a bitch finally gets his brains stomped out."

"Be a hell of a lot easier working around here," another rider opined. "He's just a pain in the ass anyway."

"Did you hear him tell Mr. Beck how he was good with horses?"

Several of the riders snickered. "The only thing he can ride is a fat whore!"

There was a muted laughter and then a rider said, "I'd rather see that blue devil win tomorrow. Be better for everybody on this ranch. One thing sure, there'll be no grievin' on my part if Elias busts his damn neck."

The other riders nodded. Not a one of them liked Elias Beck, but they all feared him and his insane temper. And either way, they had a strong feeling that either a man or a mustang was going to die come tomorrow's sundown.

5

THE FOLLOWING MORNING, the first man up on the Circle Bar ranch was the cook, but the second was young Mike Harding. Mike was standing beside the breaking pen when the sun came up just so he could admire the blue mustang stallion. He had never seen such a beautiful horse. The stallion was a tall, muscular blue roan and it had been Mike's desire for the past three years to catch and break this extraordinary mustang. It had taken all this time to finally trap the animal up at its dusty Soda Springs watering hole, and even though the stallion's mares had all escaped because the Circle Bar mustangers had concentrated on the stallion, no one was complaining. If the blue roan could be broken to ride, he would be worth a small fortune. This stallion had more speed than anything Mike had ever seen before and he'd win his owner huge sums of money on racetracks throughout the West.

"Up a little early, aren't you?" a ranch hand named Jess said, coming over to roll a smoke and hook his boot heel over the lowest rail pole.

"I can't hardly take my eyes off that horse," Mike admitted. "First time I saw him I thought he had to be unreal the way he floated across the range with his tail flying like a proud banner."

"Well," Jess said, "he's real, all right. And I got to admit that he's a good-looking sumbitch if ever there was one. But I guess you heard about what Elias plans to do."

"No," Mike said, "they all rode in long after I was asleep last night. What are you talking about?"

"Well, he vowed to break this stallion himself."

"What!"

"That's right. Got the hell beat out of him by that Shiloh fella last night in the Blue Dog Saloon."

"Well, what does that have to do with breaking this stallion?"

Jess explained about Elias and how he supposed the fool had seized upon this idea of breaking the stallion to impress his father.

"That horse will kill him!" Mike protested. "He'll get on his back and try to beat him to death like he does any horse who dares to so much as hump his backside on a cold winter morning. He puts the spurs and the quirt to the stallion and that big horse will turn into a tornado."

"I know that," Jess said. "Nobody gives Elias the chance of a snowball in hell of riding that stud horse. But he made his boast and he's going to try."

Mike groaned. He leaned his head against a rail and swore silently to himself until the stallion charged them and struck the rails. Mike and Jess jumped back.

"That sumbitch is evil!" Jess swore, watching as the stallion pawed the dirt, red nostrils flaring.

But Mike shook his head. "He ain't a bit evil. He's just plain mad. And can you blame him? How would either of us feel if someone chased us in relays about fifty miles until all our mares had fallen away and we were ready to drop? Then roped us and put a blindfold over our eyes and jerked us back and forth so that we almost strangled. I guess if that happened to us, we'd be plenty mad too."

"Maybe we would, but that don't change the fact that he'll kill Elias if he ain't killed first."

Mike sighed. He was tall and slender, with sand-colored hair, a boyish, freckled face and wide friendly smile. "Elias will ruin that stallion, even if he does ride him. I'm surprised that Mr. Beck would even allow him near the horse."

"Maybe he hopes Elias will get stomped to death," Jess said.

"His own boy?"

"Yep. He tongue-lashed him real bad again last night. Said he was the most worthless man he knew. Said terrible things to Elias. Some of the boys said it was awful just watchin' that old man speak that way to his son."

"Elias ain't right in the head," Mike said. "He never has been. Something inside of him is cruel. It didn't surprise me that he cut that whore's face up with a whiskey bottle. It'd be just like him to lose his temper and shoot this stallion to death if it piles him real hard."

Jess nodded. "The boys were talkin' late last night and we all agreed that either that horse is going down, or Elias is. One or the other ain't going to be breathin' come sundown."

"Reckon that's true enough," Mike said, moving back to the corral to peer through its heavy pine poles at the stallion. "Thing of it is, this horse didn't ask for a fight—we did."

There was a long silence as the two men watched, and then Jess turned to his friend and said, "Do you think *you* could fork 'em?"

"I don't know," Mike admitted. "Maybe but maybe not."

"Never saw anyone as good as you," Jess told him. "You're the best bronc buster any of us ever saw, but nobody has ever seen a stallion as big and strong as this one rode before. Most ranchers would just have shot the sumbitch and taken his mares."

"Mr. Beck knows that this horse is worth plenty if he's broke to ride and race," Mike said. "He's talked to me about him bunches of times."

"Elias will do his damnedest to break his spirit along with his neck."

"Elias won't last five seconds on that stallion's back," Mike said. "He'd have trouble ridin' him even if they tied one of his hooves up to his belly and the blue had to buck three-legged."

"That might be what they'll do," Jess suggested. "If Elias can't stick him fair, he'll stick him any way he can."

Mike nodded. He knew that Jess was right. There was a right and an honorable way to do things, and then there was the Beck way. Cephas was just as rough and cruel as his son, only he wasn't young enough anymore to stomp the hell out of a bad horse. And Elias was young enough but he wasn't man enough.

"If I'd have known it was going to be like this," Mike said, "I'd have drawn my pay and never helped them catch this horse. Been better off all the way around."

"Well, you're in it now and there's no getting out. When Elias goes down, it'll be your turn and the odds are still in the blue's favor."

Mike glanced aside at his friend. They had been raised up close in this rough Wyoming territory. "Jess, are you bettin' against me?"

"I'd never be stupid enough to do that," his friend said. "Why, I'd bet you could ride a Texas twister if you could just saddle the damned thing!"

Mike laughed and clapped his friend on the shoulder.

Then, his smile died and he said, "I'm glad you aren't betting for me to lose, but to be honest, I'd bet on the stallion."

"You would?"

"I would."

Jess nodded, his face set and serious. "Well," he said, finally, "first we'll just have to see what Elias can do with them Spanish spur rowels and that big old rawhide quirk he likes to use on people. It's gonna be a shame if Elias draws his gun and shoots that stallion."

"I'm not sure that I can let that happen," Mike said, tight-lipped.

"Well, how the hell do you figure to stop it?"

"I don't know," Mike said honestly. "It's just that it would be a terrible thing to shoot a horse like that. If he can't be broke or ridden, then he ought to be turned loose. At least he could breed a high-grade of mustangs that Mr. Beck could catch for years to come."

"You tell Mr. Beck that?"

Mike nodded. "Last winter we were talking about this stallion and I said that I thought he ought to just let the blue run free."

"And what did Mr. Beck say to that?"

"He told me that the blue was runnin' on his range and eatin' his grass. He said he wanted the horse either caught or shot. One way or the other. He said there wasn't nothin' in life that came free."

"He's not likely to change his mind."

"No," Mike conceded, "he's not. That's why I've got to stick on that blue until he's bucked out. Otherwise . . ."

Mike did not have to finish the sentence because his meaning was clear. "You'll stick to him," Jess said. "I remember the first time I ever saw you ride. It was old man Tattler's milk cow and when she started to buckin' and mooin', I thought I'd die laughing!"

Mike grinned. "Not me. That old milk cow had the boniest spine I ever did see on a living creature. She like to split me in half."

Jess wiped tears of mirth from his eyes. "I remember that old man Tattler almost killed us. He'd have shot you dead when he rushed out that night, only he was afraid of killin' that damned old cow."

"That's right," Mike said. "As it was, the cow stopped givin' milk. That old man hated us until the day he died."

"If you could ride that milk cow the way she carried on, you can ride that blue stallion. Maybe, if nothin' else, at least Elias will wear him down a mite."

"I don't think so," Mike replied. "I don't think he'll stick long enough, or come back enough times to do that. I'm afraid he'll just hit the dirt, go crazy the way he does, then grab a gun or a rifle and shoot the blue."

"If he does," Jess said, "there ain't nothing you can do to stop him, Mike. You try and stop him, Elias is about as likely as not to shoot *you*!"

"Yeah," Mike said, turning away from the stallion at the sound of the cook's call for breakfast.

Just before they reached the cookshack, Jess leaned close and said, "Best thing for you to do would be to ride out this afternoon on some greenbroke horse as if you was givin' it a lesson and just stay gone until after dark. That way, whatever happens, you won't have to interfere."

"I can't do that," Mike said. "I'd like to, but I just can't."

6

ELIAS AVOIDED HIS father the next morning, but he sent word that he wanted to see in private a man on their payroll named Clay Grant. Grant had the reputation of being very quick with a gun, and Elias had seen the man do a little fancy shooting out on the range one day when he'd drawn his Colt and shot the head off a rattlesnake at fifty paces. Actually, he'd shot the snake twice: once in the head, then, just for the hell of it, he'd shot the rattles off its tail. That demonstration had impressed everyone. One thing for sure, Grant was not just an ordinary rider or ranch hand. The man was an artist with a six-gun.

"What do you want, Mr. Beck?" Grant asked without any greeting or preliminaries.

"I was there the day you shot that rattler twice," Elias said. "I was wondering where you learned to use a six-gun like that."

"Around."

Elias scowled. "Around don't tell me much, Clay. What I've heard is that you were an outlaw down in Texas. Is that right?"

Clay Grant was a very ordinary looking man. He looked smaller than he actually was, and most folks would have judged him as a merchant or even a bank clerk. He had sleepy eyes, and even though he never smiled, he looked perfectly harmless. The only thing that set him apart from any of the cowboys was that he had a little nicer saddle, a better quality of boot and a newer Stetson. And a six-gun that was always well oiled and close to his right hand.

"Clay, I asked you a damn question," Elias said with impatience. "I want to know if you was an outlaw or not?"

"And if I said that it wasn't any of your damn business, you gonna fire me?"

"Maybe."

"Then fire me."

Grant started to turn and leave Elias's bedroom, but halted when Elias said, "I need a man good enough to kill Shiloh in case I get hurt on that blue stallion and can't do it myself."

Grant stopped in the doorway and turned. "Why me? I didn't hire on as a gunnie for this spread. I make a cowboy's wages."

"I'll pay you ten times what my father pays you," Elias said. "Instead of thirty dollars this month, you'll get three hundred if you kill Shiloh."

"What makes you think I'd do it for any price?"

"I don't know," Elias said. "But I spent the better part of this morning going over the list of men on the Circle Bar payroll, and something keeps telling me that you're the best one for the job."

"I got a woman and child down in San Antonio," Grant said. "I'd want the money first so that I could send it to them just in case."

"I don't believe that for a minute," Elias said. "You ain't got nobody but yourself."

"You callin' me a liar, Mr. Beck?" Grant asked in a voice that sent a chill down Elias's back. "I sure would hate for you to do that just now."

BLOOD BOUNTY

Elias swallowed. "I . . . I don't much care what you got in Texas. I'll pay half now and half if you kill Shiloh."

"Thought you wanted to do that yourself," Grant said, leaning back against the wall and folding his arms across his chest.

"Well, sure I'd like to!" Elias blustered. "But maybe it would be best all around if you did it for me. What I got to do first is ride that blue stallion."

"The boys say that horse will pile you."

"I can ride him!" Elias lowered his voice but he could not hide his mounting exasperation when he said, "Do you want the job of killin' Shiloh or not?"

"I want all of the money now."

"Hell no! You could just ride out and I'd maybe never find you."

"Two hundred, then. I'll kill Shiloh for two hundred now, a hundred when I come back to the Circle Bar."

Elias dipped his chin in assent. "How would you kill a man like that? I hear he's as good with a gun as he is with his fists. Shiloh will be a hard man to kill."

"If he wasn't," Grant said, "you'd do it yourself. I've killed hard men before. No man has eyes in the back of his head."

"Good! I'm glad you figure to ambush him."

"Only makes sense. Ain't no amount of money worth dying for." Clay Grant stepped forward and stuck out his hand, palm up. "I reckon I'll take that two hundred dollars now."

Elias had the money ready. As he counted it out, he said, "I don't want it to look like I paid you. I want my pa to think that I was going after Shiloh but that you beat me to it. So you just ambush him so that no one sees you do it. Understand?"

Grant smiled for one of the few times ever. He rolled the pile of greenbacks up in his hand and pocketed it. "I'll be back for the hundred dollars. Just don't you let that blue stallion kill you, Mr. Beck. He kills you, I'm going to have to ask your pa for the money still owed me."

Elias nodded. "If that stallion tries to kill me, I'll shoot it. Don't worry about me, Clay. Just kill Shiloh. And I'd like it even better if you'd put a bullet through his guts so he dies kind of slow."

"Might be that I'll do that," Clay Grant said just before he turned and slipped out the door.

When the man was gone, Elias lay back down on his bed. He had not looked at his face yet, nor would he because he knew how frightful had been the beating administered by Shiloh. All he wanted to do was rest, and when the sun began to slide down into the west, he'd get up and ride that blue devil of a mustang. If he could do that, then Cephas would know he'd been wrong to say such hard things about his son. Elias knew, at last, that he'd finally see respect in that ornery old son of a bitch's watery eyes.

When Elias awoke, the sun was low on the western horizon. Very quickly, he sat up and rubbed his eyes. He could hear the stallion fighting the Circle Bar cowboys and he knew that they were having a hell of a rough time getting the bastard bridled, saddled and blindfolded.

Elias didn't care. He gently splashed cool water onto his battered face and then shuffled over to his dresser drawer, where he had a very special set of Spanish spurs. Removing the silver inlaid spurs, he examined them with care and made very sure that the spurs were locked so that the rowels could not turn. That made all the difference because, locked, they would grab the

BLOOD BOUNTY 41

flanks of a bucking horse and dig in like claws, raking and tearing. Free spinning, they were largely ineffective as a method of harsh punishment. The rowels on Elias's spurs were very long and had been sharpened. This was going to be a quick, violent and very bloody encounter between him and that stallion, and one in which Elias was going to take every advantage he could in order to win.

Before he left his bedroom, he splashed water from his wash basin onto the seat of his pants. This too was an old bronc buster's little trick and gave him another slight advantage—wet pants stuck to leather and made his butt that much more difficult to dislodge.

On his way out the door, Elias looked around hopefully to see if his father would walk with him to the breaking corral, but the old man wasn't to be seen. Maybe, Elias thought, he's already out there with the boys.

When the Circle Bar men saw Elias come striding out wearing his silver spurs, they fell quiet, and Elias pulled his Stetson low on his forehead, then slipped on his leather gloves. He didn't look at the men, but instead concentrated on the stallion. He saw that Mike Harding and Jess Allard each had ahold of the blue mustang and that it was saddled, blindfolded and ready to ride.

"Mr. Beck?"

"What do you want?" he snarled at Mike.

"It's just that this is what I get paid to do!" Mike said. "I sure wish you'd let me do my job. This is a real rank horse. He's not one to fool with unless you got no choice."

"As soon as I get set in the saddle, yank the blindfold and get out of our way," Elias said. "You think you're the only one that can ride a bronc on this ranch to a standstill?"

"Well, no, sir, but . . ."

"Shut up," Elias barked as he grabbed a handful of black mane.

The stallion was already covered with froth and sweat. Its coat was shiny and yet it carried numerous scars, mementos of battles for supremacy among the wild stallions that populated the vast Wyoming ranges.

"He's scared," Elias said, feeling the big stallion tremble. "He's so damned scared he's ready to piss all over himself."

"He's mad," Mike argued. "He's mad enough to stomp you if you get thrown, Mr. Beck."

"Then I'll just have to make sure that I ride him to a standstill right now," Elias said, throwing his shoulders back and looking around for his father.

Cephas wasn't to be seen around the entire perimeter of the corral, and Elias felt a stab of bitter disappointment. After all, this was for his father to see, damn his eyes! Where was he!

"You see my pa?" he asked anxiously.

"No, sir," Jess said, trying to hold the stallion down so that it didn't rear before Elias was solid in the saddle.

"That miserable old bastard!" Elias swore as he hauled himself up into the saddle, jammed his right boot into the off stirrup and cried, "Let him go!"

Mike yanked the blindfold free and jumped back and Jess released the heavy rope that had bound the stallion close to the snubbing post. They both sprinted toward the high pole fence, and it wasn't until they were safely resting on the top pole that they twisted around and saw the blue roan driving straight into the sky. He must have already landed once because Elias's beaten face was drained and his nose was leaking blood.

When the roan came down again, it landed straight legged, the impact so jolting that it caused Elias's chin to snap down and strike his chest. The whipping of the man's neck backward as the stallion shot back up into the sky was so violent that Mike would not have been surprised had it broken even Elias's thick neck.

Once again the big mustang stallion crashed to the earth, and the cowboys sitting atop the pen all saw that this bronc was a pile-driving son of a bitch, one of the worst horses a man ever had the misfortune to ride. When the horse launched its powerful body up again, Mike saw that Elias had lost a stirrup. The man was spurring like crazy, ripping hide and hair from the stallion's gaunt flanks to leave deep furrows of blood. At the same time, Elias was trying to quirt the mustang, but now he was grabbing for the saddle horn in a desperate attempt just to stay in his seat.

Twice more the stallion bucked and by then the outcome was decided. Elias had lost both stirrups and had even dropped the rope in a hopeless effort to hang on to the saddle horn. The blue roan was still landing stiff legged and now it was also starting to spin to the right.

"He's a goner!" Jess cried.

Mike agreed and glanced sideways at the mounted cowboys just outside the gate. They had their lariats ready to throw, and they'd come dashing in on horseback to rope and pull the crazed stallion away from Elias almost as soon as he struck the ground.

The roan squealed in pain as one of Elias's spurs tore the flesh of its shoulder and then it threw the man from its back, hurling him into the poles so hard that everyone heard a popping sound in Elias's neck.

Elias screamed in pain. He seemed to be impaled on the fence, and the stallion whirled, then charged him with its yellow teeth bared. The riders shot into the corral but nothing short of a buffalo rifle could have stopped the roan as its teeth sank into Elias's chest. The man screamed again and everyone watched in horror as the stallion picked the big man up and shook him like a terrier would a rat. Dropping Elias in the dirt, the stallion reared up and came down right in the middle of the screaming, squirming man.

The scream lifted high, like it was made by a dying woman. Mike looked away just as the stallion drove its bloody hooves down again and the scream died. The mounted horsemen threw their ropes true, and before the stallion could turn and attack them, it was suspended and then driven back to the snubbing post where it was tied.

By the time the first man reached what was left of Elias, he had already breathed his last. They grabbed his boots and spurs, the vicious rowels of which were covered with blood, then dragged him out of the corral.

"Somebody get the old man!" a cowboy yelled. "Somebody go tell him Elias is dead!"

A cowboy ran off toward the house. Mike moved swiftly toward the roan stallion and, not even bothering to wait until it was blindfolded, he vaulted into the saddle.

"Cut him loose!" he shouted to the astonished cowboys still in the pen. "Cut him loose!"

One man cut the stallion loose and Mike felt his stomach drop through his ass as the stallion exploded up into the sky. A second later it landed so hard that Mike thought his neck was broke. He began to spur and ride out of pure instinct. All around him men were shouting and trying to get out of the corral before he and the stallion knocked them over.

Then Mike heard gunfire. Through the open gate of the breaking corral he saw the old man running from the house as the mounted cowboys tried to escape the pen.

"Hi-yaa!" Mike screamed, sawing on the rope and spurring the stallion toward the open gate.

He crashed into the riders. A horse and cowboy went down and the stallion stomped right over the top of them as it bolted for freedom, running like a train over anything in its path.

Everything flew past them in a blur as the stallion shot across the ranch yard. A bullet from Cephas Beck's gun grazed Mike's leg and another struck the roan in the shoulder and tore away flesh before it exited the horse's muscular body.

It was insane. The blue stallion was racing for its life and Mike guessed he was doing very much the same as a hail of bullets swarmed around him and the flying mustang.

Jesus, he thought as he crudely reined the stallion toward its home ground and the nearest Wyoming mountain range almost fifty miles distant, what the hell have I gotten myself into now!

7

WHEN SHILOH AWAKENED it was early afternoon and Josey was gone. That was fine with him. Shiloh was a man who liked to be by himself most of the time, and a woman could quickly get on his nerves during the daytime. Especially one with a busted-up face and a wagging tongue like Josey's. Still, he had found he'd very much enjoyed her during the night. She was passionate and highly skilled in her profession, and he hoped that she could manage to survive. He'd even suggested that she might go back East for a while and seek out the services of a good surgeon. She had just scoffed at that suggestion so he hadn't pushed it any further.

Shiloh was a mass of bruises so he dressed very painfully, then went over to the general store and bought himself a big bottle of liniment. The clerk who sold him the medicine was not bashful about voicing his opinion.

"You'd better limp over to the livery and claim your horse, then ride out of here, mister. The Becks will come to even the score. Maybe as early as tonight."

"I suppose that would be the sane thing to do," Shiloh drawled. "But you see, I chase men who have committed awful crimes. Crimes like murder and rape and robbery. They're men with bounties on their heads so they run. Now, I've committed no crime, save maybe being a little foolish about whipping Elias Beck. But it was self-defense and so I am innocent in the eyes of the law."

"The only law in Elk is whatever law Cephas Beck says it is," the clerk countered. "Mister, I just don't want to see anyone shot down in Elk. A killing always brings out the worst in men. They start shooting off their guns, start looking for women to rape, start thinking about getting drunk and raisin' hell. Maybe bustin' through that big glass window of mine and taking whatever they want from my counters."

"I see," Shiloh said. "Then it's not really me that you're concerned about, and not even the other good citizens of this no-account town. What you are *really* afraid of is getting this store looted."

"That and getting myself shot trying to protect it," the clerk said with more than a little exasperation.

"Well, sir," Shiloh said, uncorking the bottle of liniment and then unbuttoning his shirt, "I can understand your concerns."

"What are you doing?"

Shiloh was starting to unbuckle his belt and drop his pants. "Why, I'm fixin' to rub some liniment on myself. I took a pretty hard beating last night. That's why I'm here."

"Well . . . well, you can't undress in my store!"

"Look, I got a pair of long johns on. I ain't bare-assed. So what the hell is the matter with you?"

The clerk was mortified. "What if some respectable woman comes waltzin' in here and sees you with your pants dropped down around your ankles."

"If she's a woman, she's seen a lot worse."

"You can't do this!" the clerk cried. "Get out of here this very minute!"

Shiloh's patience was wearing thin. "Mister, you just gouged me three dollars for a bottle of liniment that probably ain't much more than turpentine, whiskey and maybe a little licorice to cut the smell. Now I'm going to put the damn stuff on whether you like it or not!"

And then Shiloh, in a moment of perversity, actually not only dropped his pants but also peeled the long johns down to his ankles.

"Good Lord!" the clerk screamed, racing to the door and pulling the shades down. "You are uncivilized! No better than a damned ignorant savage!"

Shiloh's face hardened with anger. His look was so malevolent that the clerk retreated down the aisle until Shiloh began to apply the liniment again. When he was finished, he pulled up his long johns and pants, buckled his cartridge belt around his waist, then turned to the clerk with a smile and said, "Much obliged."

Shiloh had an early supper and could not help but notice how everyone stared at his discolored face. Feeling angry, he bought a bottle of whiskey and went back to his hotel room. At least now, he thought, as he drank and watched the sunset, he could understand how Josey felt about her poor face.

Josey came again that evening and Shiloh was damned glad to see a friend. He welcomed her in the darkness with a hug and a kiss, then they wasted no time in going to bed and making love until shortly after midnight when, exhausted by their strenuous efforts, they drifted off to sleep.

"Shiloh!" Josey whispered. "Wake up!"

"Aw, no more," he pleaded, "I'm plumb worn out and I hurt all over."

"But someone is outside the door!"

Shiloh was instantly alert. He sat up and grabbed a Colt, then leveled it at the door. He could see a thin, disrupted light under the door, and when it moved he knew that Josey was right, that someone was waiting just outside.

"Maybe it's Elias come calling a little sooner than I expected," Shiloh whispered to the woman at his side. "Why don't you just slip out of the bed and get down on the floor."

Josey did as she was told and Shiloh came to his feet, gun in hand. He thought he heard footsteps moving rapidly down the hallway and he hurried to the door, then slipped the dead bolt, counted to five and ripped the door open.

The hallway was empty. Shiloh ran down it to the landing and stood there as naked as a newborn child. He saw no one.

"Hey!" he called down below. "Hey!"

A sleepy desk clerk roused himself and came out to peer up at Shiloh wearing nothing but a six-gun. At the sight of that, the clerk's eyes bugged and he stammered, "What the hell is the matter with you, mister? You drunk?"

"Hell no! Did you just see a man run through your lobby?"

"Nope."

Shiloh's brow furrowed. "Well, someone was messin' around outside my door just now."

"Mister, I think you are drunk," the clerk said. "Now you just go back to your room and sleep it off."

Shiloh pointed his gun at the man, moved his aim off him a fraction of an inch and pulled the trigger. His Colt bucked in his fist and the clerk screeched like a scalded cat, then dove for cover.

"I'll tell you one thing," Shiloh said with disgust as he remembered the store clerk, "the businessmen in Elk have got a helluva lot to learn about satisfyin' their customers. A helluva lot!"

He went back to his room and slammed the door shut, then ordered Josey back into his bed.

"Do you really think it was Elias?" she asked.

"Who else would it be?"

"I don't know, but he isn't one to sneak around like that. It's his way to bust down things and fly off the handle. If he was out there, I can't imagine him just running off like that."

Shiloh laced his hands behind his head and stared out the open window of his room at a square of stars. "Yeah," he finally said, "sneakin' around in hotels doesn't seem like it's his way at all. I wonder who else it could have been."

"Cephas Beck has a few pretty good gunmen on his payroll," Josey said. "My guess is he's hired one of them to kill you so that you can't kill Elias."

"You think so?"

"You got any better ideas?"

"No," Shiloh admitted, "I don't. But if Cephas Beck is starting to hire men to kill me, then I guess I had better ride out to his ranch and have a heart-to-heart talk with that poisonous old man."

"Are you crazy!"

"No," Shiloh said, "but I have found that it is best to face men right away and make them see the error of their ways. Otherwise, they'll keep trying to put a bullet in your gizzard."

"If you go out to the Circle Bar ranch, you'll never come back to Elk. At least not alive you won't."

"Don't bet on that," Shiloh said. "I won't wait to be

ambushed and neither will I run. I'm staying here until I get word that Harry Dawson is about and then I'm going after him for the reward."

"You don't know the meaning of fear, do you?"

Shiloh rolled over and kissed her mouth. "A fearful man isn't completely alive. I've faced death at the Battle of Shiloh when I was just a boy. I've seen soldiers, blue and gray, blown to pieces. Torn apart by artillery shells and musket balls shot by men they couldn't even see. I've seen more blood and guts than most and the only thing I fear is growing old and helpless. Of drooling and pissing all over myself the way the real old ones can do without even realizing it. That's what scares me."

"Well," Josey said after several moments of reflection, "if you ride out to the Circle Bar tomorrow to see Cephas, you sure don't have to worry about living to become old and helpless."

Shiloh chuckled and drew the woman closer. "Why don't we do it once more and then go back to sleep."

But Josey held him back for a moment. "I don't want you to die," she said, "I honestly have a . . . a fondness for you for standing up to the Becks the way you do. But you have to make me just one promise."

"What is that?" he asked suspiciously.

"Don't get killed at least until you've killed Elias. Promise me that much."

"All right," he said. "I won't get killed until Elias is dead. Now can we make love and get some sleep?"

She snuggled right up to him and she knew exactly what to do.

8

SHILOH AWOKE JUST after dawn when the first rays of early sunlight began to filter through the window curtains. A beam of light touched Shiloh's face, then slipped across the pillow to touch upon Josey. Shiloh studied the woman's face and was surprised to see that it was not nearly as disfigured as he had been told. Yes, there were scars, but they wouldn't always be red and angry. Shiloh had been wounded often enough to realize that the red puffiness he saw in Josey's face would disappear in a few more weeks.

Her nose, however, was broken and it had not been set properly so that it was bent to the right. Shiloh knew that there were skilled doctors even in Cheyenne and Denver that could re-break the nose and make it attractive again. Shiloh smiled. This was a hard but good woman. He wondered how old she was, and after several minutes decided that Josey was in her mid-twenties. She was bright and basically honest, and if given a new lease on life, she might well make something of herself yet.

Right then and there, Shiloh determined that he would have two reasons for visiting the Becks at their Circle Bar ranch. Number one, he would force a showdown, or better, an agreement so that Cephas would have to give his word that he was not sending ambushers after Shiloh. And number two, Shiloh would demand that one or both of them pay restitution to Josey so that she could have her nose and her more prominent scars attended to by a surgeon.

Shiloh rose and dressed. He liked the idea that his mission this day was not only born out of self-preservation, but also carried with it a demand for simple justice for the woman still sleeping in his bed. And if the Becks refused his demands, well, then it was far better to get the showdown over with and let the cards fall wherever they might.

Shiloh had a quick breakfast and then went over to the livery, where Walt brought out his horse. "Had him shod. He'd have thrown a shoe any day."

"Thanks," Shiloh said, reaching for a curry and then brushing the horse before he went for his saddle.

"Shoer wanted his money first so I had to cough up three dollars."

"I generally don't pay that much," Shiloh said, picking up his gelding's feet and examining the shoes. "But this is a pretty good job."

"He's the best," Walt said. "Most of my customers don't mind paying a little extra. See how he whittled down the frog a little? And note that them shoes he tacked on are about a quarter inch thicker than the average. That don't mean nothing if you leave him in the barn, but if you'll be covering a lot of miles, them extra-thick shoes will pay for themselves."

"I agree," Shiloh said, reaching into his pants for his roll of greenbacks. He paid Walt, then finished brushing his horse and saddling.

"Where are you goin' this morning?" Walt asked, trying not to sound as if he were even a little curious.

"I'm heading out to the Circle Bar ranch. People tell me the headquarters is about seven miles north on a dirt road that I can't miss. Is that right?"

BLOOD BOUNTY 55

"Why . . . why, sure! You'll catch that road just west of town. There's a big lightning-burned pine tree to mark the place, but . . . why?"

"Why what?"

"Why go out there, seein' as how Elias wants to kill you but just hasn't figured out a way yet?"

Shiloh entered Walt's sleeping quarters and, along with his carbine, retrieved a sawed-off shotgun he favored for close work. He put the carbine in his saddle boot; he'd carry the shotgun in the crook of his arm. "As for your question, I hear that Elias answers to his father."

"That's right. Old Cephas rules the roost, but—"

"Then I need to parley with Cephas," Shiloh said. "I need to explain to him the facts of life. He can't send ambushers after me and he can't let that oversized gorilla son of his beat up on women."

Walt shook his head. "Man, I think you must be crazy! I never knowed *anyone* that could tell old Cephas any damn thing. That old man won't listen to you. Instead, he'll have some of his boys draw their guns and you'll look like a sieve from all their bullets."

"Nobody lives forever," Shiloh said, climbing onto his horse with great effort because of the beating he'd taken. "But I don't believe in putting things off because it only makes them worse. And besides, there're three Circle Bar riders that put their boots to me in the Blue Dog Saloon. I sort of promised myself when I was getting stomped half to death that I'd settle a score with them boys."

"Sounds like you want to just go out in a blaze of foolish glory," Walt said. "And that being the case, would you mind giving me whatever cash you might have on you? You won't need it out there, and they'll just take it off your poor riddled body before they drag your carcass off somewhere to feed the coyotes."

Shiloh chuckled. "You sure have a way of inspiring a man to victory. You ever been a military officer, Walt?"

"Go to hell!"

Shiloh reined his horse about and rode it out of the barn. To listen to Walt and the other folks in Elk, a man would think that the Becks were invincible. Hell, Shiloh knew better. He'd whipped Elias Beck twice, and if the old man tried to have him shot or beaten, he'd either kill or whip the old man too.

Shiloh had no trouble finding the burned pine tree. He reined his horse north and was soon riding through some low, pine-covered hills. Before he'd gone a mile he saw Circle Bar cattle grazing on the mountainsides, and now and then they were joined by small bands of antelope. It was a fine morning and Shiloh took heart with the thought that not even a fool would risk dying on such a beautiful day as this. Trouble was, Elias Beck *was* a fool. Shiloh just hoped that his pa was a whole lot smarter and not so quick to lose his senses in a fit of rage.

Clay Grant stayed far back from sight as he trailed Shiloh out of Elk. He was angry for not busting into Shiloh's hotel room the night before, and angrier still for not getting a single clear shot at the bounty hunter before he'd left town. Now, however, things seemed to be moving much more in his favor. Shiloh was riding out alone, and when he turned north toward the Circle Bar ranch, Grant was first surprised and then delighted. He knew a place where he could circle around and get up ahead of Shiloh, then ambush him when he came into view. He knew a perfect place but he was going to have to ride like hell to reach it in time.

Grant was riding a strong, fast horse. It was a palomino and it served him well as he quirted and spurred the animal through the pines and over a low mountainside. He skidded down a steep game trail, jumped a stream and forced his gasping horse up through a heavy stand of aspen until he came to a pile of rocks that overlooked the road leading to the Circle Bar ranch.

He tied his sweat-drenched horse well out of sight in a spot behind the rocks. Yanking his Winchester from his saddle boot, Grant jumped from boulder to boulder until he found a place that offered good concealment as well as a clear line of fire down upon the road.

Taking a deep, steadying breath and levering a shell into his Winchester repeating rifle, he said, "I'm ready any time you are, Shiloh. Just come along nice and slow."

It was only a few minutes before Shiloh came riding into sight, and Grant flattened on the rocks and pressed his cheek against the stock of his rifle. He placed his finger on the trigger and drew a bead on Shiloh. This, he reckoned, would be about as easy a payday as he'd ever had in his life.

But behind him, his horse caught the scent of another approaching horse. Its head shot up and it whinnied. Grant saw Shiloh violently rein his own horse off the road and spur it into the pines. Grant fired, thought he'd winged Shiloh, and fired again, seeing bark fly from a tree as Shiloh disappeared into the cover of forest.

"Son of a bitch!" he swore. "Son of a bitch!"

Clay Grant hesitated. One part of him said to run, and the other part said that if he did Shiloh would just pick up his trail and follow him no matter where he tried to hide.

"Settle down!" he breathed. "Just get a grip on yourself! You're as good a man as any with a rifle. Go after the man! You winged him! He might even be down and bleeding to death!"

Grant waited anxiously for ten long minutes, and when there was no sign of his quarry, he inched back along the rock and hurried to his horse. It was all he could do not to bring the barrel of his rifle crashing down across the beast's skull. He climbed onto the animal, then whipped it around the rocks and rode about two hundred yards until he came to a heavy stand of trees beside the road. Piling off the horse, he dropped behind a fallen log and waited to see what Shiloh would do.

Shiloh did nothing. He had bandaged his upper left arm, where he'd been nicked, and then he'd tied his horse in the brush and taken a good position where he could study the rocks from where his ambusher had fired, as well as the road that stretched out between them.

Shiloh had learned that, above all, patience was the critical factor in surviving this kind of killing game. He would wait and wait and wait some more if that's what it took to bring the ambusher to him.

Noon passed and the sun glared down on the forest. Shiloh smoked quietly back in the shadows and his horse dozed through the long, quiet afternoon. Gray squirrels overhead chattered at the man below but Shiloh paid them no mind. He heard a pair of bluejays scold him and then scold each other until the sun began to slip into the western mountains. It was nearly sundown before his horse threw its head up and gazed intently toward a spot just off to Shiloh's left.

It was the ambusher. Shiloh knew it had to be, and he inched around the tree he'd been leaning up against and trained his Winchester on the spot. Two full minutes passed and then Shiloh saw the brush part just a little. Down the sights of his rifle barrel he saw a face, saw the eyes in the face widen with surprise and then terror. Shiloh pulled the trigger of his rifle and the face disappeared in a crimson splash.

He expelled a deep breath and listened to the sound of a man dying. It wasn't nice. He could hear the man's boots and fists slapping at the brush. Hear a choking sound and a deep, final sigh before total silence enveloped the forest again. When Shiloh stood up the bluejays flew away; the squirrels were already gone.

Shiloh walked over to part the brush and study the dead man. He'd never seen this one before, or if he had, didn't remember. He was nondescript but wore a real fine Stetson and pair of boots. The Stetson fit and Shiloh traded it for his own. The boots were a couple sizes too small.

Shiloh walked out onto the road and followed it up to the ambusher's horse. He untied the animal and led it back to his own hiding place. Then he hoisted the ambusher up and managed to get him sprawled across his saddle. Shiloh lashed the body down, removed the horse's bit and bridle and then sent it trotting off into the forest. Most likely the horse would eventually find its way back to the Circle Bar headquarters, and when they saw the body of their number-one ambusher, that was going to raise some hell.

Shiloh didn't care. He would already have come and gone from the Circle Bar. And if he were gunned down by Cephas and his men, then at least this way he would have the last laugh.

9

IT WAS DARK by the time Shiloh rode into the yard of the Circle Bar ranch. There were cowboys smoking in front of the bunkhouse, but none of them paid Shiloh any attention as he slowly rode his horse across the yard and dismounted. He tied up and then mounted the wide veranda that fronted the main house.

From out of the shadows a big ranch hand eased from a rocking chair and stepped toward Shiloh. "You got business with Mr. Beck, stranger?"

"I do."

The man leaned closer. He was barrel chested and a shade taller than Shiloh, and there was the heavy odor of whiskey on his breath. "You want to tell me exactly what kind of business brings you here at this hour?"

"Well, I don't believe that's any of your business."

The ranch hand stiffened. He grabbed Shiloh's upper arm. "I guess that I'll have to make it my business. So you can just do this the easy way or the hard way. Your choice."

Shiloh pivoted and in the same motion drove his knee upward as hard as he could into the man's groin. Even in the dim light he saw how the man's formerly belligerent expression was transformed into one of agony.

"Uggg!"

Shiloh's hand flashed to his six-gun and brought it up, then chopped down on the man's head. There was a soft groan and the guard collapsed in a pile. Shiloh reached down, grabbed him by the collar and hauled him along the porch into the darkest shadows. Then he went into the house and searched the downstairs room-by-room until he was satisfied that Cephas must have retired for the night in one of the upstairs bedrooms.

Shiloh tiptoed up the stairs, and the first room on his right was open with a light shining into the hallway. When Shiloh peered inside he saw a big man sitting in an easy chair with a bottle of whiskey at his side and a glass poised at his lips.

The big man's hand froze and then he slowly lowered the glass. "Who the hell are you?"

There was a slight slur to the man's voice and Shiloh reckoned that old Cephas was slightly drunk. This was confirmed when the big rancher slammed his glass down on the arm of his leather chair, splashing whiskey all over himself. "Who are you, I said!"

"I'm Shiloh. I think you've probably heard of me."

The old man blinked but, other than that, he showed no reaction. Shiloh liked that. It showed that Cephas Beck was a man who, even when half drunk, kept himself under tight control.

"How the hell did you get past Davies?"

"If he's that big barrel-chested fella that was drinking your whiskey, I gave him a little time off."

Something almost like a smile crossed Cephas's face, but it was very fleeting and it might even have been a figment of Shiloh's imagination.

"Don't worry, I didn't kill him. But I did kill another one of your gunnies."

Cephas pushed himself up from his chair. "Who?"

Shiloh described the man and then pointed to his new Stetson. "I traded him hats before he died. I didn't figure he'd mind. After all, he tried to ambush me and I suspect it was on your orders."

"I don't know what the hell you are talking about!"

Shiloh walked into the cluttered room. It had a big fireplace and a four-poster bed. There were two desks littered with papers, and on one wall there hung the biggest mounted longhorn steer head and horns that Shiloh had ever seen.

"I'll bet you brought him up from Texas, didn't you?" Shiloh said, pointing at the brindle steer.

Cephas relaxed. "As a matter of fact, I did. I was just twenty-two years old when I drove my first herd up from the Texas Panhandle country. Staked a claim on this land, and I've fought Indians, claim-jumpers and anyone else who stood between me and building one of the biggest cattle ranches in Wyoming. So what the hell have you done with your life other than beat the hell out of my son and kill Clay Grant?"

"Was that his name? No matter," Shiloh said. "He was a good shot but a little too jumpy. That and the fact that he didn't muzzle his horse before he tried to ambush me was his undoing."

"What the hell do you want?"

"I want a truce," Shiloh said. "I'm willing to forgive you for trying to have me ambushed if you'll give me your word that you'll rein in that boy of yours before I have to kill him. That, and I want enough money for a woman in town named Josey to have her nose and face fixed up right. It was Elias that busted her in the face with a whiskey bottle."

"She's just a whore."

Shiloh clenched his fists and moved closer to the old rancher. "She's a *woman*! And no man, not even a worthless son of a bitch like that boy of yours, should be allowed to bully and beat a woman."

Cephas stared at Shiloh with hard, bloodshot eyes. "Mister," he said after a long pause, "I'll give you this much, you've got nerve coming here and making your demands."

"I not only make them, I can back them up."

Cephas emptied his glass. "So can I."

"Why don't you pony up the money for the woman and then give me your word that you'll keep Elias at home while I'm in Elk."

"How much money?"

Shiloh hadn't even gotten around to thinking about a specific amount. "Oh," he mused, "I guess a hundred dollars ought to get her to Cheyenne and pay for a good surgeon."

"It's a waste of money to fix up a whore."

"That's your opinion, it ain't mine or hers. I'm not leaving without the money. That, and your word to keep Elias under a tight rein."

"Elias is dead."

It was Shiloh's turn to blink with amazement. "Dead?"

"That's right. A mustang stallion stomped him to death late this afternoon. From what you said, it happened about the same time you killed Clay Grant."

Shiloh removed his new Stetson and ran his fingers through his long, dirty-blonde hair. He couldn't quite believe this, but he was sure that Cephas was not the kind of man to lie about such a thing just to throw him off his guard.

"A mustang stallion killed him?"

"That's right. A big, blue roan that I'd been trying to catch or shoot for about five years."

Cephas refilled his glass and tossed it down. When he spoke again there was a hint of a tremble in his voice,

BLOOD BOUNTY   65

and Shiloh could see that the old cattleman was trying hard not to let this affect him, but it was.

"I'm sorry to hear that," Shiloh said. "I guess it's no secret that Elias and I hated each other and were headed for a gunfight, but getting stomped is a hard way to die."

"That boy was worthless as tits on a boar hog," Cephas said. "He never could do nothin' right. Hadn't the sense of a damn goose but he was game for a fight. He'd have fought you again, Shiloh. And you'd have had to kill him the next time."

"I didn't want to do that," Shiloh said. "And I'd rather not have killed that Clay Grant fella, if the truth be known. I'm a bounty hunter, Mr. Beck. I work for money."

"Have a drink?" Cephas asked, raising his bottle. "You won't find a better brand of whiskey between here and St. Louis."

"Don't mind if I do."

"Glasses over there on the dresser. Find one that ain't as dirty as the others and help yourself. There's plenty more where that came from."

"Much obliged," Shiloh said. "And I am sorry about your son. I take it he was the only one that you had."

"He had an older brother that was gunned down in Laramie about four years ago," Cephas said. "He was my favorite and he was smart, but he was wild. He drank too much whiskey and challenged a gunfighter."

"That's the downfall of a lot of good young men," Shiloh said. "Gunplay and drink don't mix in the same man. Never have, never will."

"Bert was fast with a gun but he was no professional. The man who killed him learned that he was a Beck and rode out of Wyoming. I hired a couple of men like you to track that man down, and they finally did in Tombstone. They killed the gunfighter and brought his head back in a barrel of whiskey just so I'd know that he was really dead."

"Huh."

"I paid those men a thousand dollars each." Cephas looked up at Shiloh. "What's the most you ever made for bringin' in a wanted man?"

"Almost a thousand." Shiloh drank the whiskey and smacked his lips with appreciation. "This is damn good stuff."

"It's the best. I have it imported from New York City. I have Cuban cigars imported from Havana. Want one?"

Shiloh shrugged. "I usually roll my own, but a cigar would be real fine."

"They're over on the dresser too," Cephas said. "Help yourself. Take a couple extra. You'll never smoke anything finer."

Shiloh took five. "How come you're treating me so good, seeing as how I shot one of your men and kicked your boy's ass twice?"

"In the first place, I didn't have anything to do with sending Clay Grant to ambush you. That must have either been his own idea—him hoping to curry my favor and get a bonus—or it was Elias's. Either way, it wasn't how I operate. If I'd wanted you dead, and my boy couldn't do the job, then I'd have come after you myself."

Cephas leaned forward in his easy chair and his voice hardened, "And don't you think for one damn minute that I couldn't have killed you man to man."

"I believe you would have tried," Shiloh said mildly as he lit the Cuban cigar, inhaled and then exhaled with a smile of pleasure. "My, oh, my, Mr. Beck. Whiskey from New York City, cigars from Havana. You do live high on the hog, don't you!"

"After Bert got himself gunned down in Laramie, I decided that I didn't have anything to save my money for. I knew that Elias would just squander everything in a few years. He'd have lost everything I'd built within five years of my passing."

"That must be a hard thing to take, knowing that all you did here was for nothing after you're gone."

"Damn right it is! But hell, after a man is dead, what can he care what happens to what he's accumulated. He's just dust."

"That's right," Shiloh said, enjoying his drink and his smoke.

They sat for several minutes not saying anything, just drinking and smoking. Finally, Cephas seemed to rouse out of his dark thoughts and said, "I got a job for you, Shiloh. One that will pay damn well."

"Sorry. I'm after Harry Dawson and his gang. That will pay damn well."

"Dawson can wait! I want you to go after that mustang."

"Why me? I'm no mustanger."

"I want you to shoot it."

"No, thanks."

"It killed my son!"

"I'm sorry. Horse shooting isn't part of my profession."

"Then how about this: The man that helped that mustang get away is wanted and there's a reward on his head of one thousand dollars."

Shiloh grinned. "Come on, now, Mr. Beck. What's this fella's name?"

"Mike Harding."

"Never heard of him."

"I swear he's wanted for murder and thievin' in these parts, and I'll personally guarantee that thousand-dollar reward if you bring him in alive to me along with the mustang."

"No, thanks."

Cephas smoked faster. "How much money would it take to get you to change your mind about bringing in Harding and that stallion?"

"Oh, hell," Shiloh said offhandedly, "I guess about twice what you're offering."

"All right." Cephas pushed himself out of his chair and trudged heavily over to a squatty little safe that Shiloh hadn't noticed. He spun the combination lock, opened the safe and stepped back to Shiloh with a pile of greenbacks.

"Here's a thousand for now," Cephas said, shoving the money into Shiloh's hands. "You'll get the other half when I get Harding and that horse."

Shiloh stared at the money. It was more than he'd ever make by killing or capturing Dawson and the worst of his gang. And with luck, he could do this job in a week or two and return to Elk in time to get a fresh lead on Dawson. Hell, he could be a pretty wealthy man before he left this part of Wyoming for greener pastures.

Cephas stuck out his hand. "We got a deal?"

Before shaking, Shiloh asked, "What makes you so sure that I won't just take all this money and ride away clean?"

"Because you believed me when I told you about how I had the man that killed my Bert tracked down to Arizona and then shot to death and his head pickled and brought back to me. Didn't you?"

"Yeah, but—"

"Then I'm counting on the fact that you know I'd do the same in your case, no matter how many gunfighters it took or how many years. No matter even if I'd die in the meantime of old age or a poisoned liver. You'd never breathe an easy breath no matter where or how long you ran."

Shiloh nodded. "Yeah, I believe that."

"Good, then take the money."

"This stallion and this Mike Harding fella. Where would I start to look for them?"

"I'll give you directions. I'll even send a couple of my mustangers along if you want."

"I don't want," Shiloh said. "I'll appreciate them showing me the general territory, but after that, I want to work alone."

"That's what I thought you'd say," Cephas growled.

Shiloh pocketed the money. "I reckon I'll be going."

"Why not spend the night in one of my empty bedrooms? If you want, I'll even share my woman with you. She's pretty good in the dark."

"No, thanks."

"Oh, one more thing," Cephas said, handing him another hundred dollars. "This is for that whore in Elk that you're thinkin' about pimpin' for."

Shiloh's cheeks burned. He had no intention of "pimping" for Josey, but he wasn't going to give this ornery old son of a bitch the satisfaction of an answer.

As Shiloh left the man, Cephas called, "You get after them first thing tomorrow, hear me! Take whatever supplies you need and however many horses. Just handle it, Shiloh!"

Shiloh entered the next bedroom with the man's words and money dominating his thoughts. He didn't like Cephas, but right now he guessed he ought to consider himself one lucky son of a bitch. For sure, this had turned out one hell of a lot better than he'd expected when he'd left Elk early this morning with Walt's dire prophecy ringing in his ears.

Shiloh bolted the door and slowly undressed. He examined the fresh bullet wound across the upper part of his left arm. There was a big full-length mirror in the room and he went over and stood before it naked. He was a mess. His body was covered with dark bruises, and he remembered that he'd vowed to settle a score with the three Circle Bar riders who'd taken such delight in stomping him into oblivion on that saloon floor.

But Shiloh decided that could wait until he'd collected the additional thousand dollars from Cephas. Revenge was sweet, but it didn't pay a man's bills.

10

MIKE HARDING HAD never ridden such a horse as the wild mustang stallion. Since breaking free of the Circle Bar he'd kept the blue roan moving without the benefit of rest. At first, he'd thought to return the mustang stallion to its home ground and turn the animal loose. Then he realized that that was exactly where Cephas would send his best gunmen. Because of losing his son, the old rancher would feel that he had to exact a revenge on both the stallion and the bronc buster who'd betrayed his trust.

Realizing his life was in danger and that he hadn't even a six-gun to protect him against those who would be sent to hunt him down, Mike had changed directions by entering a stream and using it to conceal the mustang stallion's hoofprints. He'd ridden up the stream for three miles, and it had been an adventure because the blue roan was still all bronc. In fact, if the big stallion could have gotten his neck around, he'd have torn off Mike's leg. But Mike was wary and he was savvy. He'd busted more than one big mustang stallion, and he knew their temperaments and their tricks. That's why he did not allow the stallion to eat for almost two days. By then, the toughest horse in the world would begin to tire and lose its spirit.

As he rode along, Mike had little idea what he was going to do with himself. All he was certain of was that he could not allow the Circle Bar riders to overtake him. If that happened, he and the stallion would be slaughtered. Still, he knew that he had to eat and rest himself, or soon he would be so weary that he'd make a mistake and the stallion would nail his hide.

Fortunately he came upon a cabin high in the pine-covered mountains. Mike saw smoke lifting lazily out of its chimney. There was a pole corral with two horses, and when they saw the stallion they whinnied a greeting. Almost instantly a buckskin-clad man with a leather hat, bushy black beard and a big Hawken rifle stepped into the open doorway. The Hawken, Mike noticed, was pointed right at his chest, though it was held loose and at waist level.

"Hello there!" Mike called. "I come looking for a little help. Maybe some food and a place to rest the night."

"You willin' to pay for what you want?"

Mike swallowed. He could tell that this was a rough mountain man and that it would go badly for him if he lied to the man. "I . . . I don't have any money."

"Well, what the hell you think I am, rich like a king or somethin'?"

"No, sir." Mike hauled his Barlow pocketknife out. "It's a good one," he said. "Cost me eight dollars one time in Cheyenne."

The mountain man scowled. He reached down and dragged an Arkansas toothpick from his belt. The damned thing was at least a foot long and as thick as a sword.

"What the hell I want a little bitty knife like yours when I got a real knife of my own?" the mountain man asked. "What else you got worth anything? How about that fine-lookin' horse and saddle?"

"No, sir! This is a mustang stallion and he'd kill you in a second."

BLOOD BOUNTY

The mountain man was insulted. "The hell you say! If a kid like you can ride him, I damn sure can."

"Mister, this stallion just stomped a man to death on the Circle Bar ranch. His name was Elias Beck, in case you knowed him."

"I did. He wasn't worth knowin' and I congratulate that horse for havin' such good judgment."

"Well, sir, to be honest, I sort of felt the same way. You see, I'm the top bronc buster at the Circle Bar—or at least I was until I realized that they were going to shoot this horse for stompin' Elias to death."

"You don't say!" The mountain man lowered his Hawken. "Ride on over here, boy. Let me take a better look at you and that fine animal."

Mike did as he was ordered. When he drew near, he said, "Please don't step up too close. If he decided to lunge at you and take a hunk out of your neck, there's not a damn thing I could do to stop him, mister."

The Hawken rifle came up. "He tries that, it'll be the last thing he ever does."

The stallion rolled its black eyes and tried to twist its muscular neck about so that it could watch as the man circled it with an admiring eye. When he came back around in front of the horse and rider, he said, "That's the best-looking hunk of horseflesh I *ever* laid my eyes upon."

"He's one in ten million," Mike said. "I've sat a lot of horses, but I've never seen one that can run like this stallion. Why, I think he outran the bullets that Cephas's men were firing at us when we shot out of the breaking corral and headed for the hills."

"So, that old tyrant is still alive, huh?" The mountain man thumbed back his leather hat and Mike was surprised to see that his hair was snow white. The man said, "I always expected that Cephas Beck would poison himself with greed and hatred long before now."

"He's still going strong," Mike said. "He owns most of Elk and he's pretty rich."

"But now," the mountain man said, "he ain't got no one to pass all that land, cattle and money on to."

"That's right."

"Thanks to that horse you say I can't ride."

"Maybe you can ride him," Mike said, "but I'm telling you that he's still an outlaw. He went right after Elias."

"Yeah, well, I guess that Elias deserved what he got. I can see them long, jagged hunks of hide outa that horse's flanks. I reckon Elias locked a pair of wicked spurs into that animal's sides. Cut him up pretty bad."

"Yeah," Mike said, "I've been trying to keep my heels away from his poor flanks. They must hurt something terrible."

"I got some bear grease that'd keep the flies offa him until them cuts heal. You suppose the critter will let me get near enough to slab a little on his flanks?"

"Not until he's snubbed up tight to a stout tree. Even then, we'll have to be real careful he don't cow-kick us. One blow from him and he'd break bones."

"Yeah," the man said, "I can see that. How far behind are Cephas's men likely to be?"

"I don't rightly know," Mike admitted. "My guess is that I've lost them. I rode up a stream for a good long while and I came out on gravel. I think I probably threw them off my trail, and anyway, they'll be expecting that I went off to the northeast where this stallion had his band of mares."

"Good," the man said. "Step down and let's see if we can't get this fire-breathin' son of a bitch taken care of.

I suppose I could move my horses out of that corral and put him in there."

"No, sir! He'd fly over those rails easy as pie. I'd rather tie him up to a tree, and we can feed him there if you have any grass hay."

"I do and I've also got some oats. That horse looks like he could use a feed. So do you, for that matter."

"It's been a long, hard ride," Mike admitted.

He gave his name and learned that the mountain man went by the name of Cody. Mike rode over to a tree and spent several minutes tying a big stout rope through the stallion's bridle. He tossed the rope to Cody, who wrapped it around the tree twice, then stood back. When Mike jumped off the blue stallion it tried to whirl and nail him, but Cody held the rope and brought the horse up short. In a few minutes they had the powerful mustang under control, and when they brought it a couple of armfuls of grass hay, it was so famished that it forgot about its hate of man and began to eat.

"I dunno about that horse," Cody said. "I saw the look in his eyes and I doubt that you'll ever be able to train that beast. And even if you can, I doubt you'll ever be able to trust him. Once an outlaw and a killer, they rarely change."

"You're right," Mike said. "Older mustang stallions usually can't ever be trusted. I've heard all the stories about them being ridden for years and then, one day when their owner isn't expecting it, they suddenly strike out with a hoof or their teeth and kill."

"That's right," Cody said, looking at Mike, "but you're going to go ahead and try to tame that big devil anyway, aren't you?"

"I think so," Mike said. "It sort of depends on how we get along in the next few days. If I can't make any progress with him, then I might just turn him loose, even knowing that he'll be shot sooner or later by the Circle Bar mustangers."

"Well," Cody said, "he is a fine animal, but he ain't worth dying over."

"No, he ain't. Still, if you'd have been on his back and felt his power, felt how he almost flies across the ground, well I expect you might feel the same as me and try to train him to ride and maybe even to race."

"Could be you could make some pretty good money racin' a horse like that."

"I could make a fortune," Mike said. "That's why Mr. Beck wanted to catch him instead of just having him shot. He's seen the blue run and he knows that nothing he owns can match this stallion's speed."

"You're taking a big gamble bucking the odds with that horse, not to mention going crossways with Cephas."

"It wasn't something that I planned to do," Mike confessed. "I tried to talk Elias into letting me ride the horse but he just had to try it himself. And then after I saw the way things were going to be, I just knew that I was going to run and try to get this horse out of their rifle range. I wasn't thinking about anything except running away."

"Time will make you smarter than that—if you live to be my age. But until then, let's get some bear meat into your belly. You look half starved."

"I confess that I am hungry."

Mike followed the mountain man into his cabin and was surprised at its neatness. There was even an extra bunk for him to sleep in.

"I had a partner once," Cody said, feeding his cooking fire and cutting slabs of bear meat.

"What happened to him?"

"He was killed by the bear that you're about to eat," Cody said.

Mike thought the man was joking, but he quickly realized Cody was dead serious. It would make eating the bear meat a little troublesome.

11

MIKE AWOKE TO hear the mountain man bustling around in the cabin. Because he was starved for sleep, he felt drugged and tried to drift off again, but Cody kicked his cot.

"Get up! The sun is a'risin'! There's work to be done young feller! But first, we need some bear meat to give us strength."

Mike had been taught that a man earned his keep so he knuckled the sleep from his eyes and threw aside his blanket. He could smell boiling coffee and frying bear meat. The bear meat was as tough as rawhide and so strong that it had given him the runs in the night, so he guessed he'd pass on breakfast.

"Well, Cody," he said, trying to be tactful, "I don't think that bear likes me any more than he appreciated your late partner. So I reckon I'll just stick with coffee this morning."

"You don't like it!"

"Well . . . the trouble is, it doesn't like me."

"You got a sickly stomach?"

"I never thought so until last night."

"Hmmm." Cody scowled and marched outside. He returned a few minutes later with a side of meat that looked moldy and smelled rancid. "This here is venison. It's a little gamy but it'll stick to your ribs, and I'll sear the piss and maggots out of 'er."

"I'm really not very hungry. Are those biscuits you're cooking?"

"Sure is. Biscuits and potatoes and beaver tail if you like the sound of that better."

"I do," Mike said with relief. "Though I can skip the beaver tail."

"Aw, bullshit! A man has to have some kind of meat or he's got no strength to work. Now, grizzly bear meat—just like I fed you last night—that's the best. But beaver tail will set you right."

"Fine."

Cody tromped back outside and walked a short ways out into the woods, then tossed the rotten venison into the brush for the wild animals to eat. Mike didn't see where he found the beaver tail, but it looked and tasted like the sole of a Mexican boot. It was so tough that Mike dulled his Barlow knife cutting it, but once he got it down it stayed, and the potatoes and biscuits were digestible.

"So are you going to dust off that big bastard this morning?"

"I'm going to try," Mike said. "He'll be fresh and a real sidewinder today. I might just try and get him down to a stream or a river and buck him out in about two or three feet of water."

"Well, that's kind of a chicken shit way to do 'er, ain't it?"

"Chicken shit or not, it's the smartest way. I can't afford to have that horse throw me and run away with my saddle, bridle and blanket. And without a good-sized breaking pen, that's exactly what he'd do."

"Well, what kind of a rider are you?"

"One of the best," Mike said, pulling on his boots and then buckling on his spurs. He grabbed his Stetson and headed outside.

"There ain't no running water hereabouts," Cody said, hurrying along beside him, "but there's a little lake that might do."

"How far?"

"Just a quarter mile south."

"All right," Mike said, "we'll see if we can get that blue to it before I hop on his back. But first, just getting a saddle on him again is going to be a job."

Cody scoffed at that until he saw the blue roan stallion try to twist his head around and take off Mike's arm in one bite. Failing that, because he was tied too close to the tree, the stallion squealed in fury and tried to kick Mike, but the veteran bronco buster was too wary and quick for that. It took Mike almost an hour to get a blindfold on the stallion after getting it saddled.

"Jesus!" Cody exclaimed. "That horse just purely hates you!"

"He hates *all* men," Mike said. "I don't flatter myself one bit by thinking I'm special."

"So now what are you going to do?"

"Well," Mike said, "you've got a pair of saddle horses and I've seen plenty of rope. If we each get a loop on around his neck, we can see-saw him down to that lake and take a look."

Cody wasn't real excited about the idea but he agreed, and then they finally were ready with two ropes around the stallion's neck and the blindfold securely tied across the mustang's hate-filled eyes.

"All right," Mike said, "he can't see us, and if we both keep the pressure on the ropes, we can keep him strung up right between us."

"Goddamn but I don't like this one little bit," Cody fretted. "I'd rather wrestle with a wolverine than get within reach of that horse. Why don't you just let me put a ball between his eyes? Anyone can see that he's ready to stomp another man to death."

"We won't give him that chance," Mike vowed. "Besides, he can't stomp what he can't see. Just remember that if he starts hard for me, you've got to have a good wrap on your saddle horn and stop him. Same goes for me if he makes a charge for you."

Cody took about four dallies on his horn. "I just hope he goes for you first, kid."

Mike untied the stallion, and before it realized that it was suddenly loose of the tree, Mike jumped back onto his horse and yelled, "Pull the slack!"

They both backed their horses away at the same time just as the mustang stallion reared up and charged blindly forward. It hit the end of their ropes like a runaway freight train, and the impact was so violent that Mike felt his horse leave its feet and then scramble hard to keep from being dragged to ground. Unfortunately, Cody's horse did go down. The old mountain man yelped with pain, and before Mike could help, the stallion crashed over the fallen horse and rider. Cody cried out again and Mike spurred forward. He knew that the stallion could smell the old man and would stomp him and his fallen horse into a bloody mat if he didn't intervene first.

"Hang on!" Mike shouted, leaping from the back of his horse onto the stallion's back and driving his spurs into the horse's flanks.

The mustang tried to drag its head down so that it could really buck. Mike, however, was equally determined not to allow that to happen. He sawed on the reins and kept the stallion's head chest high as the animal began to pitch and squeal like a child throwing a major

BLOOD BOUNTY

tantrum. He caught a glimpse of Cody pinned under his horse but saw no more as he struggled to master the stallion.

The roan tried to explode up into the sky and come down on stiff legs, only the footing was so slippery with pine needles that it fell twice. Each time, Mike just did manage to kick his boots out of the stirrups and jump off rather than allow his legs to be pinned or broken by the animal's weight. Each time, Mike hopped back into the saddle before the stallion could scramble back on its feet and continue bucking.

Mike fought the stallion, though he did not try to reopen its scabby flanks. He did spur, but only when the stallion bucked, and then he would grab leather and hang on for his life. Spurring, grabbing for leather and using every trick he'd learned from riding previous bucking horses, he somehow managed to stick, and when the stallion finally tired, the fight was over.

Mike rode the blue back toward Cody. "Are you all right?" he called, looking down at the man.

"Hell, no!" Cody swore. "I think I might have a busted leg like my poor damned horse!"

Mike jerked the right rein hard, bending the stallion's head back around. He tied the reins in that position and jumped off the roan's back. The stallion tried to run, as Mike expected, but it just went around in circles.

Mike reached Cody's side and the old man grunted, "Shoot this horse!"

"With what?"

"There's a Colt in my saddlebags. Shoot him!"

Mike could see that the horse's leg was broken because it was twisted at a strange angle. "I'll make this right by you," he said, checking the pistol, then pointing it at a spot just behind the horse's ear.

"Shoot!"

Mike pulled the trigger and the horse stopped thrashing. Somehow, he managed to drag Cody free and get him back on his feet.

"We need to get you back to the cabin," he said, "so that I can set that leg."

"You need to shoot that stallion first."

"No, sir," Mike said, helping the old man hobble along. "That stallion was just running blind when he bulled your horse over. It wasn't his fault. He didn't ask for all this trouble."

"You'll shoot him or I will! That stud is a man killer!"

"Just settle down," Mike said. "I take the blame for what happened."

"In that case, I'll shoot you!"

Mike helped Cody back to his cabin and eased him down on a cot. He used Cody's big knife to cut his pants leg up to his thigh, and then he carefully examined the leg.

"The good part is that it's a clean break and there's no bone showing," Mike said after a quick examination. "The bad part is that I'm afraid that you're going to be lamed up for quite a while."

"Son of a bitch!" Cody raged. "I've got traps to set and things to do!"

"I'll help you until you can get back on your feet again," Mike promised. "Right now, I've got to splint this leg. Be right back."

Mike went outside and grabbed the axe he'd seen beside Cody's woodpile. He found a straight limb on an aspen and he hacked it from the tree, then split the green wood right down the center so that he'd have a splint for each side of the leg. When he went back into the cabin,

BLOOD BOUNTY

Cody was pale, but he was more mad than worried.

"This is gonna ruin my whole damn trappin' season," he groused. "And what the hell can you do? You don't know nothing about setting traps or skinnin' out beaver or any damn thing that'd be a use to me."

"I'll learn. Either that, or I can rig up a travois and haul you down out of these mountains."

"Hell, no! What would a man like me with a broken leg do in a town?"

"I don't know," Mike said, pressing the splints against the leg and then binding them with some strips of leather that were in a big pile resting on the floor.

Cody took a swing at him while Mike was binding the leg and the blow sent Mike crashing over backward.

"I guess I deserved that and more," Mike said, rubbing his jaw and shaking the cobwebs from his head. "Now, if you don't mind, I'd better finish this job."

"I *do* mind, damn you!" Cody swore. "And I'd rather finish it up myself. Hell, boy, you're wrapping it so damned tight that it's cutting off all the circulation. My leg will go dead and rot off if them bindings ain't loosened."

"But if they're not tight enough, the bones will shift around and the splint is useless."

"I'll be the one that worries about that," Cody said.

Mike nodded and moved toward the door, but Cody's words stopped him. "Where are you going now?"

"I'm going to ride that stallion," Mike said. "Either ride him, or shoot him."

"I hope you shoot him, 'cause that will save me the bother later," Cody grumbled.

Mike went back outside and marched straight for the mustang stallion. With its head bent almost to its right shoulder, it was just moving around and around in a tight circle. Being blinded by a bandana, it had crashed into a few trees and was limping slightly, but Mike didn't waste any energy on sympathy.

As he drew near, the stallion heard him and tried to kick and bite, but Mike easily avoided its hooves and teeth and vaulted into the saddle. He reached down, untied the reins and then whipped off the blindfold, shouting, "Let's settle this once and for all!"

The stallion was already badly winded from whirling around and around in a futile effort to escape. But it still had plenty of fire fed by hate, and when Mike's spurs punched into its sore flanks, the mustang began to buck like crazy.

This time, Mike loosened the reins, let the stallion's head down and let him buck for all he was worth. The animal bucked as if it were insane, and Mike used both quirt and spurs without mercy. Each time the stallion landed on the ground Mike quirted it viciously, and each time it launched itself toward the sky Mike raked its already injured flanks until the stallion's ribs were running with fresh blood.

The fight was short and brutal. There was no quarter asked, or given. Mike knew that, if he were hurled to the ground, the stallion would kill him in a second. At the same time, he meant to punish the big horse so severely that, if he finished the battle victorious, the stallion would never again want to fight.

It ended with the stallion rearing up into the sky and crashing over backward in a last-ditch attempt to squash the man on its back. Mike had had broncs do this before, and the move did not take him completely by surprise. He jumped free, held onto his reins, and just as soon as the stallion was on its back, he kicked the horse in the ear because that was a very tender place. The stallion grunted with pain, rolled and tried to regain its footing on the pine needles. Mike kicked it again in the ear, then jumped back into the saddle, and when the horse came to its feet, instead of bucking, it just stood with its head down, sucking up great lungfuls of air.

"Is it over?" Mike asked. "Have you finally decided to quit trying to kill me?"

The stallion's ears twitched back and forth and it trembled, blood and sweat dripping from its soaked, rowel- and quirt-tortured body.

Mike clucked his tongue and rode the stallion out toward the lake where he'd originally hoped to buck the mustang out in a much less brutal confrontation. He knew the animal was thirsting for water, and when he came to the lake he let it drink all it wanted, and when it had had its fill he rode it up into the higher mountains for several hours until the stallion was behaving nicely.

"I don't know what's going to happen to you and me," he said as he reined the animal around and headed back toward the cabin. "Old Cody is bound and determined that he's going to shoot you dead. So is Mr. Beck. It seems like you've brought me nothing but trouble, while all I've tried to do is keep you alive. Guess I should just turn you loose, but that would be giving up."

Mike rode awhile in silence, his mind working hard. "What we're going to do, Diablo, is get well acquainted this summer while Cody's leg heals. By fall, if I still can't trust you, then I'm going to set you free. You'll like that just fine and you might even last a few years before one of Cephas's men puts a big slug through your lungs. But I'll leave that up to you to decide."

The stallion shook its head and moved on. Mike could feel its powerful body, and he liked the way that it watched its feet and stepped out as if it owned the mountain. Diablo had the heart of the devil and the killer instincts of a cougar, but perhaps, with enough time and patience, it might also be capable of loyalty. Mike knew that he was into this thing too deep now to do anything but give the stallion time, patience and the best horse training he could muster.

When he returned to the cabin, Mike unsaddled and heavily fed the stallion. "What we're going to have to do," he said, "is to somehow get some hobbles on you so that you can graze in the meadows around here. Otherwise, we'll go through all of Cody's hay in no time at all."

The stallion cast a wary eye at him and began to devour the hay. Even sucked up in the gut, covered with blood and sweat, the horse was a sight to look at, and Mike felt a thrill at the thought of owning, perhaps even someday racing him in small western towns. This stallion had the stuff that legendary horses were made of. It had heart, speed and wind, and just to ride into a town on its back would be a thing to make any horseman proud.

"We've cut the ties to our past," he told the stallion just before he headed back to see Cody in the log cabin, "and now there's no going back for either one of us. I know that don't make you happy, but I saved your hide and I guess you ought to think about how that means that you owe me something."

The stallion just stared at him. Mike didn't want to admit that the stallion was probably thinking about how it could stomp him to death.

12

CEPHAS BECK'S MUSTANGERS had taken Shiloh to the mustang stallion's old home ground and then Shiloh had sent them packing back to the ranch. They hadn't appreciated being sent away, but Shiloh had been adamant in his demand to be left alone to hunt the stallion and the man that had ridden him to freedom.

Over the course of three hard weeks, Shiloh rode hundreds of miles in search of the blue roan stallion. He spotted no less than seven distinct bands of mustangs, ranging in size from three horses up to eighteen. Not once, however, did he see the blue roan. He saw one band that had several foals of that color, but they were led by a big, ugly buckskin stallion that was missing one ear.

By the end of the three weeks, Shiloh was convinced that Harding had taken the stallion off someplace else to hide, or to turn loose or whatever the crazy fool intended. In a way, that kind of made sense the more that Shiloh reasoned on it. To have turned the blue stallion back to his home ground would have been asking for it to be bushwhacked by some sharp-shooter with a high-powered hunting rifle.

Now, as Shiloh left the mustang country, he faced a difficult choice. He could either abandon the hunt and return to Elk, hoping that Harry Dawson had returned, or he could give the hunt a few more days on the rather long shot that he would find Mike Harding and that killer stallion. Common sense told Shiloh to return to Elk, but he was a man who hated failure, and besides, he'd sort of gotten accustomed to the idea of having Cephas Beck's money in his pocket. If he gave up the search he'd have to give the money back, and that was not Shiloh's style.

So he rode off to the northwest, watching for signs and generally moving toward a distant mountain range. It was early one morning while riding through forest that Shiloh chanced to come across a stream, and while his horse was drinking he saw a dead beaver floating ass-end up, tail pointing downriver like an errant rudder.

Shiloh frowned, then rode his horse up to the beaver to investigate. Sure enough, the beaver had been caught in the jaws of a trap and had drowned. Where there were beaver traps, there would be men within the radius of a few miles to set and empty them, and perhaps those men had seen Mike Harding and the blue mustang. Shiloh determined that he would find the trapper or trappers, then make his inquiries. If Harding had come to these mountains, a local trapper would likely know about it.

It took Shiloh the better part of the morning ranging out in ever-widening circles before he spotted the trapper's cabin. He rode plainly into view.

"Hello the cabin!" he shouted. "Anybody home?"

"Inside!" a voice yelled. "Come on in!"

Shiloh rode forward very warily. This Mike Harding, if Cephas Beck was to be believed, was a murderer, and might very well be inside right now getting ready to put a hole in Shiloh's head. There was no sign of movement inside the cabin, and that made the hair stand up on the back of Shiloh's neck. He saw one horse in the corral and it sure wasn't the blue stallion. Still, past experience told

Shiloh that these old mossbacks that shunned civilization to lead lonely existences in the mountains were often half crazy and always unpredictable. Even if the man inside was not Mike Harding, he might be loco as a coot and have every intention of killing Shiloh just for his horse, saddle and guns.

"Hello!" Shiloh called again, reining his horse up and deciding that it would be foolish to go any closer unless the man inside showed himself. "How about comin' outside and showin' your face! You hidin' in there makes me nervous."

"Then ride the hell outa these mountains, you spooky son of a bitch!"

Shiloh reined his horse around and spurred it off into the trees. He dismounted and tied the horse, then drew his rifle out of his saddle boot. Moving fast and low, he stayed hidden from the cabin, looping in on it from behind. When he was at last beside the structure, he drew his Colt and tiptoed around toward the front door.

He waited several seconds and then was about to jump into the door with his gun cocked when a voice inside said, "How long you gonna play hide and seek, you dumb bastard?"

Shiloh grinned. "You got good ears, mister," he said, keeping his gun in his fist as he moved into view. "So why don't you come out and show yourself?"

"My leg is busted, that's why."

"Oh."

Shiloh entered the cabin, and sure enough he saw a silver-haired man propped up in bed with an old Army cap-and-ball pistol pointed in his general direction.

"Why don't we holster the hardware?" Shiloh said, slipping his own gun into his holster when the man on the bed laid his gun on his lap.

"What do you want, stranger?"

Shiloh examined the interior of the cabin. It was dim inside and his eyes had not yet adjusted from bright light outside, so he couldn't see very well, but that would change in just a few minutes. "I'm just passin' through."

"You're a damned liar."

Shiloh stiffened. "Mister, I've killed men for saying a whole lot less insulting things than that."

"So have I. Did Cephas Beck send you out here for that boy and his damned stallion?"

"So," Shiloh said, "you've seen them."

"I have." The mountain man sat up a little straighter. "The kid is my partner. I won't stand for you killing him. You can shoot his damned horse 'cause it needs killin' before it does anyone else any more harm, but you got to leave the kid alone."

Shiloh shook his head. "Cephas says that Harding is a killer and that he's wanted by the law."

"No he ain't," Cody said. "The only one that wants him is Cephas. And he'll kill the kid because he feels betrayed. I won't stand for that. I'll kill you right here and now."

"You'll die trying, old man," Shiloh said, his hand moving closer to his gun butt.

"You want to hear the straight story? Or do you want us to shoot each other?"

Shiloh expelled a long breath. "I'm listening."

"I knew Elias Beck, and if ever a fool deserved to be stomped to death by man or beast, he was it. The kid saw what an injustice it would have been to kill that stallion and so he jumped on its back and rode away."

"That's it?" Shiloh asked.

"That's it."

"Cephas says different."

"He's a bigger liar than I am," Cody said. "I suppose he's paid you cash money to find and kill that boy and his horse."

"Not to kill them," Shiloh said. "He wants them brought back to the Circle Bar."

"Figures," Cody said. "I should have knowed that he'd want to kill them himself."

"I couldn't allow that to happen," Shiloh said with a shake of his head.

"You couldn't do much to stop it if Cephas Beck had his whole crew drag iron and point it in your face, now could you?"

Shiloh had to agree. "Where is the kid now?"

"He's out checking my trap line. You see, I got hurt on account of that blue horse he has taken a shine too, even though it yearns to kill him same as it did Elias. But I'll tell you one thing, if ever there was a bronc buster who could make that outlaw an honest horse, Mike is the man."

"I'll want to wait and talk to him when he gets back."

"I expect you will." Cody raised his forefinger. "But let me tell you something, mister, you'll take that boy back to Cephas Beck over my dead body."

"Whatever," Shiloh drawled. "But whatever I decide to do, you'll be one of the first to hear about it."

Cody nodded. "You like bear meat?"

"Not particularly, but I'm not in any position to be particular right now, am I?"

"No," Cody said, "you are not. There's some bear meat in the smokehouse around in back. Why don't you use that big knife to cut us a slab and fry it on my fire. Mike don't like bear meat, and the stuff is going to rot 'cause I can't eat it fast enough, and I already threw good venison out to the animals."

Shiloh nodded and went outside. He found the smokehouse, and when he opened it he was nearly blinded by a swarm of flies and the stench of rotting meat filled his nostrils. He slammed the smokehouse door shut and went back into the cabin.

"Your bear meat is rotten. I've got some salt pork in my saddlebags that I can boil up for us."

"Be a nice change," Cody said. "I'm gettin' tired of bear meat and beaver tail."

Shiloh went outside and gathered an armful of wood for the stove. Within an hour, he and the old mountain man were eating pork, beans and potatoes.

"I would have thought all the beaver was trapped out of these mountains years ago," Shiloh said.

"They were, almost. Then they came back over the last twenty or thirty years. Not much of a market for their pelts now, but it's enough to buy supplies and live on from one year to the next. I ain't complainin' none."

"Never helps anyway," Shiloh grunted. "How come Harding stayed?"

Cody looked up at him. "It's like I said, he's a good kid, and since that damned stallion was the cause of my current misery, he felt duty bound to stay. Now, would the kind of an outlaw and murderer that old Cephas described do that for a hurt man?"

"Not likely."

"Well, see then! You kill or take Mike back to the Circle Bar—either way he ends up dead—and you'll be the death of an innocent man. You got any conscience, Shiloh?"

"Some."

Cody nodded. "I hope so. 'Cause if you oppose me and that boy, my conscience will be clear when I blow a hole through you."

Shiloh gazed into the mountain man's eyes and knew he wasn't bluffing.

13

IT WAS LATE in the afternoon when Mike Harding finally appeared on the blue mustang stallion. Cody and Shiloh were sitting outside next to the cabin. The mountain man's leg was resting on the earth warming in the sun and he was reminiscing about the days of the free-spirited mountain men when Mike reined the stallion up and looked down at them.

"Afternoon," Mike said, his eyes flicking nervously between Shiloh and Cody. "Howdy, mister."

"Howdy," Shiloh replied, coming to his feet. "That sure is a fine-looking stallion you're riding. He looks as if he could run like the prairie wind."

"He can," Mike said, patting the stallion's powerful neck. "He's a mite obstreperous yet, and I'd be lying if I said he was trustworthy, but he's got more speed and heart than any horse I've ever ridden."

"That's not exactly what Mr. Beck says about him," Shiloh said, carefully studying the young man's face in order to read his reaction. "Mr. Beck says that this horse is a killer. Says he wants him back."

Mike looked at Cody for help, and finding none he squared his shoulders. "As you can plainly see, stranger, I'm not even packing a gun. But I'll fight you with fists or knives before I'll give up this animal to Cephas. He'll just kill it, and he won't do it quick with a bullet. He'll make this stallion suffer. I couldn't abide with that."

Shiloh began to roll a cigarette, concentrating on it and giving himself a few extra moments to consider his response. "Well," he said when he'd lit the cigarette, "I couldn't rightly allow Cephas to torture a fine animal like that either. But he's paid me some big money to bring you and that horse back to his ranch. If I don't do it, I'll have to return the man's money, and I sure don't want to do that."

"Then keep it and ride on," Cody drawled from off to one side. "Cephas has more money than he knows what to do with. He won't miss what he gave you."

"Yeah," Shiloh said, "that's what I keep thinking. But I also keep reminding myself that I'm a professional and I do have a code that says that I earn what I get paid."

"We all got to do what we got to do. I'd just hate to see us dyin' over a little disagreement."

"So would I," Shiloh said, moving a little closer to the stallion.

"Mister," Mike said, "I'm askin' you not to get too near this horse. He's not real nice to people and he might just take your arm off clear up to the elbow."

Shiloh studied the handsome animal, and he could see that the young man knew what he was talking about. The stallion's ears were laid back and it's black eyes sparked with defiance. Shiloh looked up at the kid. "So how come he lets you around him?"

"He wouldn't if he had the choice," Mike said. "But we've sort of come to a hard understanding. I don't use my quirt or spurs and he don't try to kill me. So far, it's working out just fine."

"That may well be," Shiloh said, "but that horse comes off Cephas Beck's range and therefore is rightly his to claim."

"No sir! This horse is wild and belongs to nobody. As far as being on Circle Bar ranch land, well, I can tell you for a fact that Cephas don't own this stallion's home ground. Where he came from is just scrub pine and sage. It's danged near worthless for cattle and it'll never be claimed except by sheepman. That won't happen, however, as long as Mr. Beck is still alive. He hates sheepmen even worse than he hates someone like me who he figures betrayed him."

"Didn't you?"

"No sir! I hired on to break wild horses, not to see them shot for bein' themselves. I've always told Mr. Beck that if we caught a stallion that couldn't be rode or tamed, I'd want to set him free."

"And he agreed?"

"He did," Mike said. "Could be the fact that I never had a horse that I couldn't break that had something to do with his thinking, but when this stallion came along, we all knew it was going to be something special. I begged Elias to let me handle this horse. But no sir! He got his back up and he wouldn't listen to nobody. He just climbed on and went to war with this stallion. Everyone knew that only one of them would come out of that breaking pen alive."

Shiloh nodded. "I get a feeling that all three of us are glad that it was that stallion that won."

"I am," Cody said. "That Elias Beck was a fool and a trial to everyone he ever met. I say good riddance."

"I can't honestly say that I disagree," Shiloh said. "I fought Elias twice and whipped him both times, but they were hard fights and I knew that he'd keep coming back until he figured a way to either beat or kill me."

"So," Cody said, "what are you going to do, mister? I won't let you take Mike and that stallion back to Cephas just so he can satisfy his lust for blood and look big in front of his cowboys."

Shiloh smoked in silence. He looked up at Mike and said, "Cephas Beck told me that you were a murderer. He said that you'd killed men and were wanted by the law."

"No sir!" Mike argued. "Look! I'm not even packing a gun! All I am is a good horse breaker. I worked for Mr. Beck for a good many years breaking the worst horses you can imagine. I've never had a minute to spend practicin' with a gun."

"I'm inclined to believe that," Shiloh said.

"You should be," Mike replied. "After all, if I was a gunman wanted for murder all these years, why did Mr. Beck keep me on his payroll right up until the moment this horse stomped his son to death?"

"I should have asked him that question myself," Shiloh confessed.

"He'd have had an answer," Mike said. "He's old but he's sharp and quick-minded. He'd have given you some reason. But the truth is, I just jumped onto this stallion's back when I saw what was going to happen and I raced off."

"What are your plans now?"

"I hope to stay alive and maybe train this stallion until he can be trusted to race on the dirt tracks, where I can surely earn a pile of money."

"Maybe you could use a manager," Shiloh said. "Someone who knows how to collect winnings."

Mike blinked. He stared into Shiloh's eyes and found himself nodding his head. "Yes," he whispered, "I sure could use a manager. Interested?"

"I'm interested in anything that pays good money," Shiloh said.

Cody sighed with relief. "Well, then, I guess we can stop bandying around and open the jug of corn liquor I been savin' for a celebration."

Shiloh nodded. "You want to come along?" he asked the mountain man.

"Nope. But by and by, I could use a little extra money now and then. Not much, but just enough to account for the fact that I'm slowin' down some and the beaver is gettin' scarce in these parts. Been trappin' here more'n sixteen years now, and I'd hate to leave my cabin and start over somewhere else."

"I'll see you get a share," Mike said, "even if it comes out of my own pocket."

Shiloh didn't say anything. The old man had saved the kid's life, not his. And if the kid wanted to pay a debt, that was just fine. "Fifty-fifty. Right?"

"All right," Mike said a little reluctantly. "Although it seems to me that since I saved Diablo and broke him to ride, I ought to have a bigger share—providing we can get him to run."

"Fifty-fifty," Shiloh repeated firmly. "Otherwise, I might just have to take you back to Cephas."

"Just you try it!" Cody growled.

"Now hold on!" Mike shouted before angry words came. "Fifty-fifty is okay with me. Shiloh's job of collecting the winnings is the hardest and most dangerous. I reckon that he probably deserves half."

Shiloh relaxed. "How soon can we leave?"

"I'll need another month to work with this horse. I can't train him to race against anything but our own animals, and then just back and forth across one of these meadows. But I think that he'll come along pretty fast with your help."

"Then we'll start training him tomorrow."

"Well," Mike said hesitantly, "I can't tomorrow."

"Why not?"

"Because he's got to check my trap lines," Cody said gruffly. "They have to be checked and reset and the beaver pelted and brung in for tannin'."

Shiloh scowled. "I don't rightly see how we can be horse trainers and trappers at the same time. A man has got to do one thing or another—but not both unless he does 'em half-assed. Leastways, that's my feelings."

"I don't give a damn about your feelings," Cody grunted. "Them trap lines has got to be taken care of come hell or high water. And since my damned leg is busted and I can't do it, you and Mike have got to do it for me."

"He's right," Mike said.

Shiloh was not pleased. "For how much longer?"

"Until the snow flies next winter ought to be it," Cody said smugly.

"The hell with that noise!" Shiloh said. "Now where is that jug of corn liquor? Either we start drinking and get along, or I'm likely to call the whole damn thing off and take the horse back to Cephas."

"Help me up and inside," Cody ordered. "Rest me on my bed and then let's get down to some serious drinkin'. We'll cook up some bear meat and—"

"Oh, no!" Shiloh protested. "To hell with your bear meat! The liquor will be all my stomach can handle."

"I agree," Mike said, dismounting and walking Diablo over to tie the animal up before returning to help the old mountain man inside.

Cody's lip curled down in disgust. "I do declare," he said, "you young ones ain't got no stomach for livin' wild. You'd have made piss-poor mountain men, both of you."

"I think we've just been insulted," Shiloh drawled.

Mike allowed himself a boyish smile. "Yeah, we have for a fact. Old Cody has a sharp tongue on him."

While the old man fussed and cussed, they hauled him to his feet and dragged him inside, then laid him on his bed. "It's buried under that pile of hides over there in the corner," Cody said, pointing with his finger.

Shiloh unburied the jug, and from its considerable weight he could tell that it was clear full. He uncorked the jug, laid it on his right elbow and drank. The corn liquor was hotter than chili peppers and it seared his gullet and made his tongue curl and grow hair.

"Whoo!" he wolfed. "Who in blazes made that poison?"

"I did," Cody said proudly. "And I can tell by the way your eyeballs are smokin' that you liked it just fine."

Shiloh took another pull that made his toes tingle. "Ahhh!" he choked, passing the jug to Mike, who took it hesitantly.

When the kid drank, his cheeks blew out and his eyeballs bugged. He spat the liquor all over the floor, threw the jug up in the air and whirled to race outside. Shiloh caught the jug and began to laugh with Cody.

The mountain man finally managed to say, "I don't think that boy is going to want any more, do you?"

"I sure don't!"

"Good! We can get royally drunk and have a high old time swappin' lies."

Shiloh didn't know about having a high old time, but he did notice that the first two swigs of the corn liquor had fired in him one hell of a thirst.

They drank hard and in silence for nearly fifteen minutes before Cody said, "Tell me something, Shiloh. Are you a hired gunfighter?"

"Nope."

"Then what? You ain't no cowboy. I can see that by the way you ride and act."

"I'm a bounty hunter," Shiloh said after a few minutes. "I hunt men that have crossed over the law. I take a bounty on bringing them back dead or alive."

"You're worse than me," Cody said. "I just kill animals for their fur."

"We're the same," Shiloh said. "I kill animals too. Only difference is they ain't got fur and they're missing a couple of legs."

Cody guffawed and drank. He wiped his mouth with his sleeve and looked out the door but could not see Mike. "I like that kid. You see that he's taken care of, hear me?"

"I'll do my best," Shiloh promised. "But I can't promise anything. You know that."

"Yeah," Cody said, "I know. But as long as you do your best then I won't have any complaints no matter what."

"Shut up and hand me the jug," Shiloh ordered. "And we can talk about how much money you're going to need to stay outa our hair."

Cody grinned. "I like the way you get right down to the fact of the matter without fartin' around."

"So how much?"

"Five hundred a year ought to do it if you're makin' a lot of money off that stallion."

"You'll get ten percent for doin' nothing."

Cody thought on that for a minute and then stuck out his hand. "I reckon," he said, passing the jug to Shiloh, "that we have ourselves a deal."

Shiloh took the jug and said, "There is one little problem."

"Cephas? Hell, just avoid the man. Leave Wyoming! You can find dirt-track racing anyplace you go out West."

"There's another thing."

"What?"

"I gave my word to a crippled man that I'd find and bring in the man who shot him in the back. It was Harry Dawson. I mean to kill him or watch him hang."

"Even I've heard of Dawson," Cody said. "He's got a gang, ain't he?"

"Yep. That's what brought me to Elk in the first place. It's one of his favorite towns."

"It's Cephas Beck's town," Cody said pointedly.

"I know," Shiloh said. "And that's the little problem I was mentioning."

Cody's brow furrowed and he did not look pleased. "You just take care of that boy and win us some money. As for Dawson, shoot him in the back like he did that other fella. Do it so nobody sees you."

"Don't matter if they see me or not," Shiloh said. "I already told everyone in Elk that I was after Dawson."

"Now, why did you do a dumb thing like that?"

"Wasn't dumb," Shiloh snapped. "Dawson is the kind of man who has too much pride to walk away from a challenge. If he hears that I'm looking to nail his hide, he'll have to come to Elk."

"Mister," Cody said, taking back his jug, "you've got too damn many irons in the fire and you're going to get yourself burned. Now, I don't mind that one damn bit, but if you allow that kid to get burned too . . ."

"I won't," Shiloh promised. "And as for Cephas, I'll just go back to his ranch and return his money. I'll tell him that I learned the truth—that the kid isn't wanted by the law and that he's done nothing to deserve trouble. As for the horse, well, I'll just let old Cephas know that this is one thing he can't have no matter how much money he pays."

"And do you really expect him to accept that, just because you say it has to be?"

"No," Shiloh admitted, "I guess I don't."

"You'll have to kill Cephas and a few of his gunnies. And then, supposin' you survive that—you'll also have to kill Harry Dawson and all of his men. Shiloh, I don't think you're that damn good."

Shiloh pulled on the jug and the liquor didn't burn at all anymore. "Mister," he said in a raw voice, "you may not think I'm that good, but there are a lot of dead men that know different."

Cody blinked and decided to keep his mouth shut and get stinking drunk.

14

THE NEXT MORNING, Shiloh awoke feeling as if his brain had been beaten with a stick and his eyes had been thumbed inside out. Cody looked even worse and Shiloh dimly recalled that the old rascal had foolishly revealed that he'd had a second jug of corn liquor that needed emptying.

Shiloh staggered outside, hands pressed to his temples. He stood swaying in the bright sunlight, and he tried to keep from losing his gorge and wondered if he'd been fool enough to eat some of that rotten bear meat that Cody was pushing.

Shiloh couldn't rightly remember when he'd gotten so roaring drunk. Not for years. Not since after the nightmare he'd endured at the Battle of Shiloh when he'd stood, half-man, half-boy, and seen how artillery could blow the heads off fighting soldiers, and seen how they'd still kept moving just like decapitated chickens. Or how men could still kill with a missing arm spurting their life-blood away. Yes, he'd drank like a man insane after that battle, but nothing had exorcised the devils in his mind and, in fact, they had become more hideous.

But last night, the dream of that terrible battle had not reappeared in the swirl of his alcohol-drugged mind, and it had been a good drunk, a happy, funny and satisfying drunk. Until this morning.

Shiloh found an oaken bucket and filled it from the little spring behind the cabin. He doused his head again and again until he could think and see clearly. It was a cool morning and he saw that Diablo and Mike were already gone, and then he recalled that they were checking the old man's trap line.

Shiloh squeezed the water from his hair and face, then staggered inside the cabin and found his shirt. He finished dressing, then buckled on his .44 caliber Army Colt and found his Stetson.

"Where the hell are you goin'?" Cody growled.

"To find Mike and that horse."

"They'll be back come nightfall."

"Maybe."

Shiloh went out to his horse. He felt awful but knew that a few hours of hard riding would do wonders if it didn't kill him in the process. He saddled his horse and rode out knowing the general area where Cody was running his lines. It wasn't far, no more than five miles in the next canyon over. And it wasn't that Shiloh expected the young bronc buster to run out on him, but more that Shiloh needed an excuse to get some fresh air and be by himself until he was fit company.

Shiloh pushed his gelding very hard all morning and did not come upon Mike and the stallion until well past noon. The big mustang was tethered to a pine tree, and when it saw another horse it bugled a challenge that the gelding flatly ignored.

"Howdy!" Shiloh called to the young bronc buster, who was up to his knees in water setting a beaver trap. "Doing any good today?"

"Naw," Mike said, "only three so far. There aren't many beaver in these rivers anymore."

"How does Cody get by?"

"He hasn't said so," Mike replied as he carefully set the trap baited with beaver scent and a fresh twig, "but

I think he just plays at trappin'. I think how he really makes his money is from pannin' gold."

"You serious?"

"I discovered some gold pans he'd hidden from me. He'd buried them out behind the cabin, but some animal had dug 'em up. Anyway, I think it's gold that keeps him going, not beaver."

"I expect you are right," Shiloh said, dismounting and coming over to study the sandy streambed. "Beaver pelts aren't worth much of anything anymore. I've heard that eastern women buy them for their fur shawls and such, but they like ermine and silver fox better. So you just play along with the old man's game?"

"Why not?" Mike asked. "I'm the reason he's hurt and we've become good friends. I'm going to hate to leave him when we go horse racing."

"You think that stallion will put up with it?"

"Yeah," Mike said, "more and more I do."

"I hope so."

For the rest of that afternoon, Shiloh trailed along with Mike. He didn't offer to help set the traps, skin out the additional pair of beaver they found, or tend to Diablo, but he did keep the young man company. He found that, like Cody, he enjoyed the bronc buster. Mike was good natured, pleasant and intelligent, and he sure knew a lot about mustanging and wild-horse breaking.

"There are two ways, bustin' 'em hard, or takin' it slow and breakin' 'em gentle. Most ranchers just want you to do it fast and get onto the next horse. Hell, it doesn't take a lot of talent to bust a bronc. All you got to do is stick in the saddle and hurt him worse than he hurts you. When he gives up, he's broke. You got to put a rein on him and teach him a few fundamentals, but those are things that even a man like you can teach."

"I suppose so," Shiloh said, ignoring the insult.

"Now I tried to break Diablo gentle but it just didn't work. He's too strong and too old and set in his ways. When he was two or three, it would have been different. But after a stallion is four or five on up, and after he's had a band of mares to boss around, he won't take to gentling. He's mad clear through and through."

"I can't blame him one damn bit," Shiloh said. "I'd feel the same way myself."

"And so would I," Mike said agreeably. "But that doesn't change the fact that I still have to break him. It just makes it that much tougher."

Shiloh studied the restless stallion. "I'll bet he weighs a good twelve hundred pounds and every ounce of it muscle."

"That's a close guess," Mike said.

"Do you think you'll ever be able to trust him with your life?"

"I don't know." Mike wiped blood from his hands, finished skinning out the last of the beaver and carefully rolled up the bloody pelt and jammed it into a leather sack. "But I'd say probably not. A horse like that will never forget what it was like running wild and free. It's bound to be angry inside."

"I guess," Shiloh said, remounting his horse and waiting for Mike to do the same.

Mike came in from the side and sawed the stallion's head around toward its right shoulder so that it could not bite him as he mounted. The animal didn't really attempt to bite the rider, but Shiloh could see that it was thinking about the idea.

It was way past dark when they topped the ridge and headed back down toward the meadow and the cabin.

BLOOD BOUNTY

There was a full moon out, and it was so bright that it made the stars look pale by comparison. A great horned owl sailed on silent wings across the meadow, and they saw it dip down into the tall meadow grass and screech with delight as it carried a flopping varmint up into the highest branches of a nearby pine tree. They heard a sharp, abbreviated squeal and knew that the varmint was meat.

When they came within sight of the cabin, Mike said, "That's odd."

"What?"

"No light in the stove or even a candle. Cody likes to work on his traps and make things out of leather in the evenings."

"Well, he's probably not feeling up to his usual ways," Shiloh said without elaborating.

"Yeah," Mike said, "I can see what you mean. You and him really bit the hair of the wolf last night. When I went to sleep, it was well past midnight and you two were going full steam. Singin' and a-carryin' on like wild men."

"Like mountain men," Shiloh corrected. "He knows a lot of fine old songs I never even heard of. 'Course, all of them are bawdy, the kind you would never sing in the church."

"Of course."

They rode on into the yard and the cabin was silent. Shiloh dismounted, and since Mike would take a little while to settle Diablo in for the night, Shiloh unsaddled and turned his horse loose in the corral and headed for the cabin.

It was as he walked across the dark yard that something strange hit him quite forcibly. He halted and scratched his head. Nothing seemed especially wrong that he could see and yet . . . what was the matter? Why were his internal warning bells clanging louder and louder?

All of a sudden Shiloh realized he was looking down at the tracks of a shod horse that was not his own. And since neither Diablo nor Cody's horses were shod, that meant that an outsider had come to visit this day, maybe even several outsiders.

Shiloh raised his head and stared at the cabin, which now seemed forboding. If there were strangers inside, they'd be watching him very closely now, and probably with drawn guns or else they'd have been calling out a greeting upon his arrival.

Shiloh decided that he had better not try to turn away too suddenly or he might just get his hide riddled with bullets. That being the case, he had only one choice and that was to continue on as if everything was normal. He was wide awake now; no haze of the night before remained and his heart began to pound.

He moved forward as if everything was just fine, only when he came to the door, instead of going on inside, he suddenly dove sideways along the front wall. Instantly, muzzle flashes and the sound of gunfire split the night air. He heard curses and more shots and then he dragged out his own gun and sat up against the wall, gun pointed at the doorway.

"Cody!" Mike shouted, dropping an armful of hay and starting forward. "Cody!"

"Get back!" Shiloh bellowed as more shots erupted from the dark interior of the cabin.

Mike hit the earth, rolled over twice and managed to get behind the wood pile just as a gunman pushed outside the cabin.

"Freeze!" Shiloh ordered.

The gunman twisted around, his eyes searching too high for Shiloh, who calmly aimed at the gunman's chest and pulled the trigger twice. The gunman slammed over backward.

"Hoyt!" came a shout. "Hoyt, are you all right?"

"He's dead!" Shiloh cried. "And so will you be in about five seconds unless you and anyone else you brought throws your guns out."

Shiloh heard two quick shots and then threw himself belly-down into the doorway and opened fire. He heard the impact of his slugs striking flesh, a sound he had heard far too many times before. Shiloh kept pulling his trigger until his hammer slammed down on an empty cylinder. He rolled out of the doorway and held his breath, listening.

There was no sound from inside. "Cody!"

Silence.

Shiloh jumped up and ran inside. He couldn't see worth a damn and tripped over a body. Spilling headfirst onto the dirt floor, he cussed and yelled at Mike to light a match and come inside. A few moments later, by the light of a candle, they found two dead strangers and one dead old mountain man.

Mike dropped to his knees and wept like a baby. "Why?" he cried. "Why did they do it?"

Shiloh knew exactly why they'd killed the old man. They'd killed him because they knew he'd try to shout a warning. Shout to tell him and Mike that two more gunmen had been hired by Cephas Beck to come and gun down Mike Harding and bring that stallion back for a killing.

15

IT BEGAN TO rain hard sometime late in the night. Over the mountains lightning split the sky and stabbed down to pierce the rocks and the tallest forest trees. When it did, the earth howled as if in pain and the ground shook and thunder rolled like cannon fire.

Shiloh had his dream again that night, the terrible dream of the dead and the dying. Of headless bodies moving ghostlike with black liquid fountains spurting up from their trunks. Those with heads were just as hideous. Their eyes burned and their mouths were contorted into horrible silent screams. They all seemed to gravitate toward Shiloh as if, somehow, he was their only salvation. Or at least had some answer to why, why the death and the rendering of minds and bodies. Why the slaughter and the suffering. *Why?*

Shiloh was lifted out of bed by his nightmare and the crashing of nearby lightning. Through the cabin's doorway he saw a pine tree ignite like a pitch torch and then sizzle in the night and belch white smoke into the rain.

Shiloh was drenched in his usual fear sweat and he could not sleep. He fed the stove, dressed, brought in more wood and fed that too until the stove banged in cherry-red protest.

"You can't sleep, huh?" Mike said, lacing his fingers behind his head. "You must be thinking of Cody and how he died, too."

Shiloh hadn't been thinking of Cody but saw no reason to admit the fact. The truth of it was he didn't want to think about the old mountain man, who had been lashed to his bed and then tortured before being shot twice in the head. Shiloh figured that the dead men hired by Cephas had tortured the old mountain man trying to learn the whereabouts of him and Mike and the stallion. Obviously, Cody had refused to tell.

"Yeah," Shiloh said, "he was a good man."

"How can you be sure that Mr. Beck hired that pair?"

"Because," Shiloh said, "why else would they be here? Who else but Beck would have paid them enough to come this far and go to this length to get us?"

There was a long silence, and then Mike said, "So what are we going to do?"

"I think Cephas has to be held responsible for Cody's death. I think that, if we let this pass, the man will send others. He'll keep sending them until someone kills you, me and the stallion."

"Maybe I should have let them kill the stallion. Or at least . . . at least freed him to return to his home range and fend for himself."

"Maybe, but you didn't, and now we are marked men," Shiloh said. "Cephas probably figures I betrayed him the same as you did. He didn't know I intended to return his damned money. But that's finished now. It's us . . . or him."

Mike sat up. "You mean you think we have to kill him?"

"I don't know of any other way short of him dying of natural causes before he sends others after us. Do you?"

"No," Mike said quietly. "But I'm not a gunfighter. I've never killed a man before. I'm not even a very good shot."

"Well, you'd better start practicing," Shiloh said.

"I don't have a gun."

"Use one of the dead men's," Shiloh said, trying to mask his rising sense of exasperation.

"But . . ."

Shiloh's patience snapped. "Listen, there's a time to fight and a time for peace. Against Cephas, there can be no peace and we have to kill that old snake before he has someone kill us."

"You make it sound so damned simple."

"That's because it is simple," Shiloh said. "A man can get in big trouble if he starts to make things more complicated than they really are. What we have to do is kill Cephas, and then we can get on with our lives. Racing horses and going after Harry Dawson and his gang."

"I don't know how you can do it."

"What?"

"Talk about killing people like it was the weather."

Shiloh listened to the roll of thunder as it crashed and caromed back and forth across the mountain peaks. "After being at the Battle of Shiloh," he heard himself say, "killing a fella now and then just isn't all that troublesome anymore. I saw *thousands* die in the space of two or three hours."

"But that was war!"

"Life is war!" Shiloh snapped. "And if you haven't figured that much out yet, you aren't going to make it. Not with that stallion and not with surviving Cephas Beck and his hatred."

Mike stared at the fire in silence and Shiloh fed it some more wood as the storm and the night dragged on toward a cold, dismal dawn.

In the morning they buried Cody out in the meadow and used kerosene to burn the bodies of the two hired men along with the cabin. They did not even bother to take the pelts or beaver traps, but left them to scorch in the ashes.

As they saddled and mounted their horses, the cold, steady rain began to fall again. The lightning had moved off to the west, but that did nothing to raise their spirits.

Just before leaving, they turned to watch the roof fall and they could hear the burning timbers sizzle as ash turned to mud and ran across the yard like small, dirty ribbons leading into the meadow.

"There aren't but a few left like Cody," Shiloh said, glancing back toward the mountain man's unmarked grave. "He's one of the last of the breed."

"I don't even know if he had any kinfolk we should notify."

"He didn't," Shiloh said. "He'd cut all ties with the past. That was the way he'd wanted it to be. It's finished except for what we have to do to even the score." Shiloh looked at Mike. "I know you're a bronc buster and you've told me that you're no good with a gun. But can you hit what you aim at with a rifle?"

"Yeah, but . . ."

"Then here," Shiloh said, drawing out his Winchester and handing it to the man. "All I ask is that you don't panic and you don't quit on me in the middle of a bad fix. If you want to quit now, give me back the rifle and git while you can."

"I couldn't do that," Mike said, after a long pause. "I'm the one that brought the grief on Cody. It was me that was the cause of his leg gettin' busted and them two killers putting slugs in his head. If I'd never passed this way, he'd still be alive and healthy."

"Probably," Shiloh agreed. "But what is done is done.

BLOOD BOUNTY

That old man, if he could come out of the grave, would tell us that he wouldn't rest easy until we settled the score with Cephas Beck. Cody said that Cephas had already lived way too long."

"Sounds like you've already made up your mind to kill him."

"I pretty much have," Shiloh said. "I've seen his type before. They think they can play God and they somehow come to believe that they have the power of life or death over other men."

"Doesn't a bounty hunter think that way too?"

Shiloh gripped his saddlehorn. "No," he grated, "not an honest one. You see, many is the time I've risked my life to bring a man to justice when the easiest, the most sensible thing would have just been to shoot him and deliver his body to the authorities for his reward. Instead, I bring them in if they will mind their manners. I bring them in and let the law decide whether or not they're to live or to die. The only law that Cephas Beck believes in is his own."

"Yeah," Mike said, mounting the stallion. "I've worked for the man long enough to know that. I've seen him tie men to a post and strip them to the bone with his bull whip."

"He's had them shot, too," Shiloh said. "It was obvious that he was perfectly willing to have me kill you if that was what it took to get this stallion."

"For a fact?"

"Yep. And I can also say that we are both dead men if we don't settle with him first."

"But just to shoot him down," Mike said, shaking his head. "I can't abide by that. And how would we get off that ranch without the others killing us?"

"I don't know."

"You don't know?"

"No," Shiloh admitted. "Most often what happens is that you take one step at a time and play the cards as they fall."

Mike mounted the blue stallion. "I dunno," he said, reining the horse south. "What you're proposing to do sounds like we are just asking to get ourselves killed."

"I disagree." Shiloh rode after the young man but was careful not to let his gelding get within striking distance of the mustang stallion. "Experience tells me that we either kill that man or he kills us."

"So you keep sayin'."

"Are you with me in this?" Shiloh asked pointedly. "And I mean with me all the way however it goes."

"I'm doin' it for Cody."

"You can think that," Shiloh said drily, "but what you won't admit is that you are also doing it for yourself because you know that Cephas is out to put us six feet under."

Mike didn't say anything, but Shiloh knew the bronc buster's mind was turning to his own way of thinking. Mike had watched Cephas long enough that, if he were honest, he'd have to admit that nothing short of killing the old varmint was going to save their own hides.

"Shiloh?"

"Yeah?"

"You consider yourself a lucky man?"

Shiloh frowned. "That's a strange question to ask."

"Maybe. But do you?"

"Not particularly," Shiloh said after a moment. "If I ever decided I was lucky, I might stop being so careful. And if I did that, then I wouldn't last very long in this profession."

"So why don't you take up another profession?"

"Like what? I can't farm and I won't work in a mine. I'm not a bronc buster like you and I can't swing a loop worth a damn so I wouldn't be worth a damn as a cowboy."

"Be a sheriff. Or a United States marshal."

"Nope. A sheriff has to put up with too much bullshit from the townspeople who pay his salary. A marshal has to stay in one territory. I like to travel around too much. I like to decide who I am going after and who I choose to let someone else take in for the bounty on their head."

"You like the freedom."

"You bet," Shiloh said. "And if we start to make some money racing that stallion, you'll come to understand some of the same."

Mike nodded and they rode on in silence. It grew dark but the rain stopped falling as they rode steadily south toward the Circle Bar ranch and a showdown that could not be avoided.

16

WHEN THEY RODE into the Circle Bar ranch yard, Mike said, "It doesn't look like anyone is here except the house stall and ranch hands."

"Where does the old man keep his horse?"

"In that barn."

"Let's take a look," Shiloh said, reining off in that direction.

They rode up to the barn, and when it was determined that Cephas Beck's horse was gone, they rode back to the ranch house.

"Hello the house!"

A man stepped out onto the porch, and when he recognized Shiloh and Mike he went for his gun. Shiloh beat him handily.

"Be a real poor decision," Shiloh said. "No sense in you dying a fool, is there?"

The man shook his head and raised his hands shoulder high. "I see you brought 'em both in," he said, looking at Mike and the stallion. "Mr. Beck is going to be real pleased about that."

"Good! Where can I find him?"

The man hesitated and Shiloh's voice took on an edge. "I asked where he went."

"He went into Elk last night. Said he'd be back by tonight. Told the cook to have dinner waitin'."

"What's for dinner?" Shiloh said, dismounting.

"Now wait a minute! You can't just invite yourself in!"

Shiloh tied his horse to the hitch rail and looked up at Mike. "I reckon we could both do for a bath and a good meal. Maybe a cigar and a glass of some of the best whiskey you ever tasted in Mr. Beck's parlor."

"Now I can't let you do that!"

"Mister," Shiloh said, waving his six-gun in the man's general direction, "I want you to start walking north and don't you stop."

"What?"

"You can come back tomorrow," Shiloh said. "By tomorrow, things will be quiet again. But the best thing for you—and anyone else on this place other than the cook—is just to git. You understand me?"

The man nodded. "Mike," he said, looking up at the bronc buster, "you're going to regret you ever saw this man. You're gonna regret it to your dyin' day."

"Maybe so," Mike said, dismounting, "but I got to play out the hand I was dealt. So why don't you and whoever else is inside just do as Shiloh says."

In a few minutes, everyone was out of the ranch house and following a trail north.

"They won't go but a mile or two before they stop and then come sneaking on back," Mike said.

"That's just fine," Shiloh said. "Let's hide our horses around back and go inside and make ourselves at home."

"Mr. Beck will kill us when—"

"He'd kill us anyway, remember?" Shiloh said quietly.

Mike nodded and they took their horses around behind the house and then went inside and helped themselves to a glass of Cephas's best whiskey and his Cuban cigars.

"Relax," Shiloh said with a grin as he enjoyed his drink and smoke.

BLOOD BOUNTY

"How can you possibly relax? Mr. Beck and his men might come riding in here any minute! And if they do, there will be a fight! And if there's a fight, we're probably going to die!"

Shiloh could see that the young bronc buster was upset. "Here," he said, pouring the man another glass of whiskey, "drink this and settle down. We didn't come here to get ourselves killed. Leastways, I didn't."

"But—"

"Even Cephas can live through this if he says the right things," Shiloh decided out loud. "It's all up to him."

"Aw, shit!" Mike lamented. "There's no use in talking to you! You don't seem to understand that we're going to get riddled with bullets!"

Shiloh pretended not to hear. "I want you upstairs when they return," he said. "You can be in Cephas's bedroom and I want you to have that rifle trained on his chest. I'll brace him and whoever else is with him when they show up. You keep out of sight just inside that window either until the shooting starts, or until I holler. Is that clear?"

"Yeah, but . . ."

Shiloh's voice hardened. "The thing is that I've done this business before. It's never quite the same, but it's still predictable once you know the kind of man that you're bracing."

"Oh, yeah! Well I know Mr. Beck and he won't back down an inch!"

"Of course not," Shiloh said calmly. "If he did, I might let him live. But he won't . . . so you kill him."

"Me?"

"That's right. You put a rifle bullet through his lungs and I'll go after the others. If I can beat them to the draw—and I ought to because they'll be caught off guard by your shot—then they might just decide to throw down their guns and ride away with their lives."

Shiloh managed a tight smile. "You sure do look flighty, Mike. Why don't you go upstairs to Cephas's room. I'll have the cook bring up a bath. You can soak yourself and drink a little more whiskey. Take four or five of these cigars and enjoy yourself."

Mike shook his head. "To tell you the truth, I'm kind of hungry right now. I'd rather eat."

"Then call in that cook and have him dish us up whatever he was preparing for Cephas! Hell, now that you mention it, I'm sorta hungry myself."

After dinner, Shiloh had the cook brew them a pot of coffee and he sent a cup upstairs for Mike. Shiloh walked over to the stairwell and called, "I'm going to sit in that fine rocking chair on the porch and wait. You all right up there?"

"Sure! About as right as any condemned man can ever be!"

Shiloh shook his head and muttered, "I hope that young fella has a little better attitude about broncs."

There was a fancy gun case in the parlor and Shiloh knocked out the glass front of it and removed a beautiful English shotgun, probably used for pheasant or some such genteel kind of game. He had no trouble finding a box of shells and he loaded the weapon, then carried it outside and eased down in the rocking chair, but not before he'd pushed it back into the shadows.

The rain was gone and the stars were shining bright. Shiloh lit another of Cephas's fine cigars, kicked his boots up on the porch railing and laid the shotgun across his lap.

"Any time, Cephas," he said out loud, listening to a frog croak down by a little fishing and stock pond fed by a silvery stream.

He did not have long to wait. Before the cigar was half finished, Shiloh heard the sound of running hooves. "They're coming!" he yelled up at the moon. "Just stay back out of sight but be ready."

"We're dead men," Mike called down in a hollow voice, "but don't worry, I'll back you to the end."

"Have another whiskey," Shiloh called. "Might raise your flagging spirits."

Shiloh ground the butt of his cigar out with his heel, then removed his Colt and laid it on his lap. He cocked the hammers of the shotgun and thumbed back his Stetson. A few minutes later, what looked to be about a dozen riders came hauling in. It was not hard to see the thick form of Cephas Beck in the lead.

The old man dismounted and handed his reins to one of his men. He coughed and started up the porch steps as the riders turned toward the barn and corrals.

"Evening, Cephas," Shiloh said when the rancher was almost to the front door, "nice night for a ride."

The old man had been reaching for the door, but at the sound of Shiloh's voice he whirled and stared. "Who's that?"

Shiloh eased himself out of his chair. The riders had not heard him yet and that was all to the good. He said in a low voice, "It's Shiloh. Remember me? I'm the one that you paid a lot of good money to bring back Mike Harding and that blue stallion that killed your boy."

Cephas stiffened. Shiloh could not see his old face clearly, but could tell from the way that Cephas tightened in the shoulders that he was tensed, ready to go for the Colt strapped to his side.

"I sure do think that you'd better reconsider your plans," Shiloh said. "Better yet, why don't you and I mosey back into your parlor and have a little more of that fine whiskey and a cigar. We got some important things to talk about."

"Did you kill Harding and bring me back that stallion?"

"No."

"Then we've got no business at all," Cephas said. "And furthermore, I want my money back."

"Well," Shiloh drawled, "there is a little problem with that. I decided to keep some, and give the rest to Josey so she could get her face fixed. 'Member Josey? She's the one that Elias busted across the nose with a whiskey bottle a couple of months back."

"You son of a bitch!" Cephas hissed. "I'm going to have you strung up by your balls! I'm going to whip the hide off of you so clean you'd think you were a damn skinned buck instead of a man. I'm gonna—"

"You're going to do nothing but listen," Shiloh interrupted. "Either that, or you're going to die."

"Boys!" Cephas roared. "Come back here!"

"You just made a real bad mistake," Shiloh said. "Tell 'em never mind."

"Go to hell!"

Shiloh sighed. "Those two men you sent looking for me and Mike, well, they killed a good man up in the mountains. He knew you, Cephas."

"What was his name?"

"Cody. He said you'd lived too long."

Cephas snorted with derision. "Cody was a no-account old windbag! He never amounted to a hill of beans. I took the only woman he ever loved and I used her! That's why he didn't like me."

Shiloh hadn't heard that story, but he thought it was probably true. "You're a mean son of a bitch and you really have lived too well too long."

One of the men in the yard called out something in question. Shiloh said, "Tell them to go away."

"It's Shiloh, boys!" Cephas shouted. "I reckon we're going to have us a little more fun tonight after all."

"Kiss your big ass adios," Shiloh said, leveling the shotgun at him.

"I'm an old man," Cephas said, "and you're still young. I get the best of the dyin'."

"You would," Shiloh hissed, "except that I don't plan on dying young."

Cephas barked a coarse laugh and went for the gun at his side. It was dark but not so dark that Shiloh could not see the gun come up, and when it cleared leather, he pulled the trigger of the shotgun and had the satisfaction of watching Cephas take a load in his big, overstuffed belly. The man screamed. From out in the yard, men shouted and all was confusion. Someone opened fire from the yard, which was crazy because it would have been impossible to distinguish Shiloh from Cephas where they stood in shadow. Cephas took a bullet in the side and fell heavily.

Shiloh heard the banging of Mike's Winchester from up in the window. Men scattered in the darkness, cursing. Shiloh dashed into the house. "Mike! Let's get out of here!"

The bronc buster came busting down the stairs, eyes wild, rifle smoking in his fists.

"Back door to the horses!" Shiloh ordered.

Mike did not need either urging or directions. He flew down the hall and was first out the back door to find Diablo raising hell. The stallion lashed out at

Mike with a back hoof and missed, but bit him on the thigh as Mike untied the horse and swung into his saddle.

"Let's get out of here!"

Shiloh and Mike took off racing and the blue stallion left Shiloh's horse as if it were dragging an ore wagon behind. Shiloh had never seen anything run so fast in his life.

They ran for five miles before they drew their horses up and let them blow.

"I can't believe that we're still alive!" Mike whispered, breathing as hard as if he had run the five miles himself.

"Well, we are," Shiloh said. "I told you we'd come out of it alive."

"You shot him, didn't you."

"With his own shotgun. He was hit once or twice by his men. I left him on the porch dying."

Mike was silent for several minutes. "So what happens to us now?"

"We go into Elk and wait. My guess is that the men on the Circle Bar payroll will fight it out among themselves for the spoils. They're jackels who long ago sold their pride and honor for their jobs."

"You don't cut them much slack, do you?"

"No," Shiloh said. "Sooner or later every man has to make a stand or just give it up. You made your stand when you defied Cephas and rode off on that stallion. The men back there gave up or sold out. That's the difference."

"You think they'll come to Elk looking for us?"

"They'll come to Elk but I'd bet anything that they won't say a word. Why should they? They'll have stripped the house of everything of value. You think about it and

BLOOD BOUNTY   131

you'll realize that they owe us a favor. Leastways, that's the way I see it."

"I hope they see it the same," Mike said. "There's a few men that were on that payroll that I used to call my friends."

Shiloh said nothing. It had given him no satisfaction to kill Cephas Beck, even though it was justice that the old rancher had to pay for being the cause of Cody's death. Cephas had been ruthless and a killer himself. He'd fathererd a vicious, brutish son and the whole damn lot of them were poisoned.

"What are we going to do next?" Mike asked, his voice suddenly very weary.

"Well," Shiloh said, "I'm going to try real hard to get a lead on Harry Dawson, and you're going to start training that stallion to race. I've never seen a horse that could run like that!"

Mike brightened. "He was really something, wasn't he? I felt like I could almost outrun bullets."

Shiloh grinned. "If that horse wasn't so damned ornery, I'd be jealous and want him for myself. By the way, how is your leg?"

"Leg?"

"Yeah," Shiloh said, pointing to the kid's bloodied pants. "Don't tell me you are still so excited that you don't feel what that killer horse did to you?"

Mike stared at his leg with amazement. "Well I'll be damned! I didn't feel it! I still don't!"

"You will," Shiloh said confidently. "By the time we get to Elk, you will."

17

MIKE WAS IN pain by the time they reached Elk and Shiloh had to help him up to their room. He bought some liniment at the general store and a new pair of pants, too.

"You ain't going to die of a horse bite, I can promise you that right now."

"Good! My leg is all swollen up like a pickle."

"It'll be fine," Shiloh said. "If there was a doctor in this town I'd bring him over, but there isn't much of anything he could do except charge us money."

Shiloh reached into the sack he'd brought up. "Here's a bottle of whiskey. A pull or two on that wouldn't hurt any."

"Thanks," Mike said. "Where are you going now?"

"I'm going to see that our horses are taken care of and then I'm going to get something to eat. Maybe see a friend named Josey. Want me to bring you something up here to the room?"

"No, thanks. I'm feelin' too bad to be hungry. Well, maybe I could eat a tin of peaches or some beef jerky. Or a piece of apple pie from Buster's Café along with—"

Shiloh grinned and opened the door. "You're going to be just fine." His grin faded. "I left that six-gun by your bed for a reason, you hear? If anyone knocks, you make damn sure it's me. Anyone else, you better tell 'em to go away."

"So you do think that Mr. Beck's men might come to settle the score."

"I don't think so, but I don't want your death on my conscience. So you've been warned and armed. Just be alert. I should be back in a few hours at most."

"You going to be askin' for Harry Dawson and his gang?"

"Sure."

"Why don't you just let it go," Mike said. "You decided to keep all that money that Mr. Beck paid you. Ain't that enough?"

"It's never enough," Shiloh said. "Like most, I've got an endless list of wants and needs. I need a new saddle and rifle and some new clothes. I need a pretty woman and a faster horse. I need to see more of the world than the hard side of these damned frontier towns. I got wants that would take a day just to list out loud."

"I got wants too," Mike said, "but I could rattle 'em off in about a minute."

Shiloh started to leave but his curiosity got the best of him. "All right. One minute."

"I want to win over that blue stallion so he don't try to kick, bite or stomp me. I want to win a lot of money racin' him and find myself a pretty girl to marry and spend it on and I want to buy some fancy clothes. I want a good dog and one honest friend who likes to go fishin' and I want to live to grow old and see my children have children. That's what I want."

Shiloh was touched. "Those are all good and honest things, Mike. I doubt that you'll ever be able to trust that blue horse 'cause he's a killer at heart. And as for a dog, why, they're all over the place. People runnin' 'em off wherever you go. I do hope you find a good woman to marry but I don't agree on spendin' all your money on her. Money spoils a woman something awful. I've seen it happen more than once. Keep your woman happy but humble. Keep her with children."

"I'll remember that," Mike said as Shiloh turned and went out the door.

Shiloh's first stop was to see Josey, and when she recognized him she rushed into his arms and kissed him on the mouth. "I was afraid that I'd never see you again!"

"Aw," he said, "I told you that I'd come back. How have you been?"

"Fine. As you can see, I no longer hide in the dark, but I'm not much to look at anymore."

Shiloh reached into his pocket and retrieved a wad of money. He peeled off almost the full thousand dollars and handed the bills to Josey.

"What's this for?"

"A surgeon. I think one can fix your face up just like new. It ain't bad now, but it'll be real pretty again."

Josey kissed his mouth and hugged him again. "You have the reputation of being a hard man, Shiloh."

"I'd prefer to keep it. I guess you can figure out why."

She nodded. "I suppose I can. I won't even say where this money came from."

"I want you to leave Elk and not come back. Use some of that money to get yourself a fresh start in Denver or maybe even back East."

"If I went back East, I'd never see you again."

"I pass through Denver now and again. I could look you up."

"Then that's where I'll be," she decided out loud. "Now, will you stay with me until I leave?"

"I can't."

"But why?"

Shiloh heaved a deep sigh. "I killed Cephas Beck. He drew his gun on me, but I'd have killed him even if he had not. Thing of it is, there might be a few men with enough gumption and loyalty to the old man's memory to want to settle the score. If so, I have to be ready and I don't want to be worrying about you."

"I can take care of myself."

"Then do it," he urged. "Take the next stage out of Elk going to Denver and find that surgeon. Give yourself a new face and a new name. You can buy respectability with enough money and I've given you enough for a while."

"And then?"

"Start a business of your own—other than what you did before," he added quickly. "Or find a good husband and think about raisin' some strong children."

Her lips brushed his cheek and her hand slipped down his hard, flat belly. "You ever think about having children, Shiloh?"

"Nope."

"Not even a little?"

Shiloh swallowed. This woman really knew how to make a grown man sweat. "Well, maybe the idea has crossed my mind once or twice," he admitted.

"Then why don't we go to bed and talk about it?"

Shiloh couldn't remember a single reason why not, so he guessed it would not hurt to spend a few hours here with Josey before she left in the morning. He could start asking all over town about Harry Dawson tomorrow.

18

WHEN SHILOH RETURNED to his hotel room the next morning, Mike was gone. He'd left a scribbled note on the bed which read: "Since you didn't come back and I didn't want to starve, I went to eat."

Only after reading the note did Shiloh realize he'd completely forgotten to return with food for the young bronc buster. Shiloh was tired enough from his night of pleasure to want to take a long nap, but he headed back outside instead and went down the street looking for Mike.

He found the young man eating a hearty breakfast at Buster's Café. Shiloh ordered a breakfast of his own, and as soon as the coffee arrived and he'd swallowed a few gulps, he said, "Sorry about not bringin' you supper last night."

"That's okay," Mike said. "I got by, but when you still didn't show up by early morning, I figured I had better find my own way down to a feed."

"How's the leg?"

"Sore but that liniment helped. How was Josey?"

"She helped, too," Shiloh said with a small grin.

"I'll just bet. You moving in with her and leavin' me at the hotel?"

"Nope."

"Why not?"

"Josey's leaving for Denver this morning."

"How come?"

Shiloh hesitated because he really did not want to get into the whole story about how he'd helped the ex-prostitute with money for a surgeon and a new start in life. "Guess she just got an itch to move on."

"And you didn't scratch that itch a little last night?"

"Shut up and eat your breakfast before it gets cold," Shiloh ordered.

They were still lingering over coffee almost an hour later when three Circle Bar riders came galloping into town, and damned if they didn't tie their horses up right in front of the café.

"That's Bonner, John and Hank!" Mike whispered. "They'll recognize us in a second if they come in here!"

"Are they gunfighters?"

"No, but . . ."

"Then I doubt they'll want to fight," Shiloh said, pushing his chair around and making sure that his Colt was loose in his holster. "Just have that pistol you're wearing ready to use."

"But you just said—"

"It always pays to be prepared for the worst," Shiloh said calmly as he drained the last of his coffee and watched through the window as the three men finished tying their horses and came inside.

The three did not see Shiloh and Mike until they were seated at a table near the front. And when one did recognize Shiloh and Mike, he jumped to his feet so suddenly that he knocked his chair over backward.

"It's them!" he cried, hand fading toward the gun on his hip.

Shiloh's gun was up first and Mike's wasn't all that far behind. Shiloh cocked back his hammer and said, "I think you'd just better settle back down at that table and order your breakfast, friend."

The other two sat frozen, their faces hard masks. Finally, one of them raised his hands and said, "I ain't workin' for Mr. Beck no more, Shiloh. You got no cause for killin' me."

"I don't mean to kill you or your friends," Shiloh said. "I just want you to know that I'm willing to put the past behind. What happened at the ranch is done. Is that how you three boys see it?"

They exchanged glances, then the first one said, "We're quit of the place. Took some things instead of the pay that was due us, then we rode out. The others are still fightin' over the house, cattle and every damn thing they can try and lay claim to. There's already been one killin' since you and Mike left. There will be more. We wanted no part of it."

Shiloh lowered the hammer on his Colt. "I'm glad to hear that. Enjoy your breakfast."

Shiloh paid for both breakfasts, then he and Mike filed out, nodding to the three cowboys as they passed.

"You still got that blue killer mustang?" one of them blurted just as Mike was leaving.

Mike turned. "I've got him and I mean to keep him."

"After what he did to Elias, I can't understand why you'd want to do such a foolish thing. You got more horse sense than that."

Mike opened his mouth to say something, then closed it and walked out following Shiloh, who said, "Why didn't you answer the man in there?"

"I dunno," Mike said. "I wanted to, but keepin' that stallion *is* foolish and I ought to know better. Thing of it is, I just never had a horse that good of my own and I probably never will again. I'd hate to give the stallion up, Shiloh."

"Once," Shiloh said as he walked and Mike hobbled along on his bad leg, "I had a bad woman that I loved."

"Why?"

"What do you mean?"

"I mean, if she was bad, why did you love her?"

"I loved her for the same reason you love that blue horse."

"I don't understand."

"She was fast and fun to ride."

Shiloh hooted at his own little joke and Mike blushed. They moved on down the boardwalk with no particular place they wanted to go.

"Let's go in here," Shiloh said, stepping through a pair of batwing doors as he entered the Blue Dog Saloon, which was just opening up and still empty. They were greeted by Joe.

"What can I do for you, Shiloh? Last time you were here, I thought you were going to get kicked to death."

"I still owe you one," Shiloh said. "But what the hell are you doing here? Last I heard you were seen leaving town."

"That's right," Joe admitted, "but it came to me that running wasn't going to solve anything. So I turned right around and came back; and now I'm just biding my time till Cephas Beck or his men come for me."

"I guess I might as well be the first to tell you that I had to kill Cephas Beck in self-defense."

"What?"

"That's right. And as far as I can say, a lot of businessmen in Elk have reason for celebration. I'd say you are finally your own boss, Joe."

"Jaysus!" Joe whispered. "You killed Cephas!"

"I did, though it gave me no pleasure. Well, maybe a little."

Joe pulled out a bottle of whiskey. "This calls for a celebration! Drinks on the house! All you want for a week!"

"Maybe one for me," Shiloh said. "I'm full of coffee."

"Nothing wrong with that! You can be drunk and wide awake at the same time."

"I'm sure you can," Shiloh said, "but what I really want is to find Harry Dawson and collect the bounty on his hide and that of his men. Have they come through since I've been gone?"

Joe shook his head. "Shiloh, you are a most amazin' man! You tell me you killed old Cephas, the biggest thing that has ever happened in this part of the country, and in the same breath you are asking about Dawson, wondering if you can kill him too."

"I'd still take him in alive if he surrendered and gave me his word he wouldn't try to escape before I collected the bounty."

Joe shook his head. "You are one of a kind, Shiloh. One of a kind."

"Well, thank you, I guess. Now what about Dawson?"

"As a matter of fact, he and his boys did ride through town about three or four days ago. They stopped at Darla's whorehouse, but she stood them off with a shotgun and wouldn't let them inside. They rode on to Pine City."

"How far is that?"

"About thirty miles. But they'll likely be back. Last I heard, there were only two girls working in Pine City, and they were so ugly that their smiles would give most men the shingles. Everyone wants Josey to go back into business but she won't. Things are pretty grim."

"More girls will come once they hear about men with money and a need."

"The need, now you got that right, but I don't know about the money." Joe poured himself another drink. "The thing of it is, with Cephas dead, everything changes in Elk. Who do you think will take over his ranch?"

"I have no idea. He's got no relatives, just a crew of vultures. My guess is that they'll strip the house, barns and Circle Bar ranch of everything."

"You're probably right," Joe said. "I wouldn't be surprised if a lot of folks from town rush on over there in hopes of getting in on the spoils."

"If you want my advice," Mike said, "you'll stay right here. Bonner just said that there's already been fighting among the men and at least one is dead."

"Hope they don't all kill themselves off," Joe said, "that bunch is pretty good drinkers. I need their business."

Shiloh and Mike stayed about an hour. Two more customers came in, and as soon as they heard that Cephas was dead they rushed out to tell others.

"It's a damn good thing that old man didn't have a single friend in this world," Joe said. "Otherwise, Shiloh, you'd have yourself a passel of enemies."

Shiloh nodded, his eyes distant. He turned to Mike. "Now that it's clear you don't have to worry about someone gunning you, I think I might just head on over to Pine City."

Mike was silent for a few minutes. "You want me to come along?"

"No," Shiloh said, "I'd rather you stayed here and worked with that horse we're going to race and get rich with."

Mike could not hide his relief. "I'll do it," he promised. "And if you come back—"

"Not if," Shiloh said, "when."

"Right. When you come back, we'll go racing."

Shiloh liked that just fine. He tossed down the rest of his drink and bid the pair farewell.

"You ought to stay right here in Elk!" Joe called. "You could be mayor or any other damn thing you wanted to be! Your name will go down in this town's history."

"Big deal."

"Well, it is a big deal. We might even rename Elk Shiloh!"

"Don't even think about it," Shiloh said, turning as he reached the doors. "I don't want this sorry one-buggy collection of shacks named after me."

"Well, all right!" Joe shouted, trying to supress a grin. "To hell with you! Maybe I'll claim to have shot Cephas and they'll name it after me! Joe Root!"

"Root'd be fitting for this dirt-poor town," Shiloh said on his way out the door.

After he was gone, both men stared at the door for several minutes. Joe finally shook his head and said, "Ain't he a piece of work though!"

"He is."

"Tell me exactly how Shiloh killed the old man. Don't leave out a thing."

Mike poured himself another whiskey, and since he was not a regular drinking man his eyes were already starting to get bright and a little glassy. "Actually," he said, burping loudly, "it was *me* that killed old Cephas."

Joe's eyes widened with disbelief. "Aw, come on now!"

"It's the truth," Mike boasted. "Shiloh just backed me up."

"You don't mean it!"

"I do." Mike frowned with concentration. "If I can convince you that I'm telling you the truth, do I get free drinks for a month?"

"Damn right! *You'd* be the hero, not Shiloh."

"And maybe they'd rename this fine town Harding?"

"Well, maybe so. Harding, Wyoming, has a nice ring to it. I don't see why not."

"I'll make a fine mayor," Mike said with a lopsided grin. "But it wasn't easy killing old Cephas. He was tough and he was crafty. Almost like a father to me, he was."

Mike waxed on and discovered that he was a pretty good liar when he had the drink running strong in his veins. Shiloh, on the other hand, went over to the stage line office, where Josey was sitting under a cottonwood tree with a ticket in her hand.

"You look pretty," he said, noting her new dress, the yellow bonnet pulled low over her face and the way her blue eyes showed hope that hadn't been there for years.

"I knew you'd come to see me off," Josey said. "I knew I hadn't seen the last of you."

"I'll see you again in Denver," Shiloh promised. "You just find yourself a respectable boardinghouse for ladies and I'll find you."

"For ladies," she whispered. "I ain't no lady."

"You are now," Shiloh said, taking her hand. "You are as much a lady as any I've known."

"Then you never met even one," she said quietly.

Shiloh was about to admit that he had not, but his voice was drowned out by the arrival of the stage.

"We're runnin' behind schedule!" the driver called down. "So, ma'am, if you're gonna use that ticket, you'd best hurry up and get on board."

Shiloh helped Josey into the coach and kissed her good-bye. He waved as if he were a dutiful husband wishing his wife good-bye on a short trip, and when the stage was gone he turned and headed for the livery and his horse.

Shiloh's smile was gone now. He was going to Pine City to look for Harry Dawson and he was prepared to use his gun.

19

SHILOH RODE INTO Pine City just after sundown. He found a livery and then inquired about a room for the night.

"You can bed down in one of my stalls for a quarter a night," the liveryman told him. "Or you can pay a dollar and bed down in a tent on a tick mattress on the ground next to ten or fifteen other men that'll snore so loud that you can't sleep."

"I'll take the stall, but I want it bedded down with clean straw," Shiloh said.

"Why, sure!" The liveryman held out his hand. "Be a dollar altogether for you and your horse."

Shiloh paid the man. "You wouldn't happen to know where Harry Dawson is staying, would you?"

The man crammed the dollar into his pocket. "Nope."

"But he has been in town." It was not a question.

"Yep."

Shiloh curbed his urge to grab this man by the gullet and shake him. "Where did he go?"

"Mister, I got no idea about where anybody comes or goes and I just keep to my own damn business. It's a whole lot simpler and a damn sight healthier that way."

"Yeah," Shiloh said, "I suppose it is at that."

He left the livery and found a café. It wasn't much but the food was better than he'd gotten at Buster's Café, and the apple pie he had for dessert was as good as he'd tasted in a long, long time.

After supper, he moseyed into one of the two saloons in town and ordered a whiskey. There were only about eight or nine men in the place and none of them were playing cards.

"New in Pine City?" the bartender asked.

"Yeah. Just rode in today. I'm an old friend of Harry Dawson. I heard that he was in town."

"Is that right?"

"Well, don't you know?" Shiloh asked.

"Come to think of it, there was a fella by that name that rode into town a few days back. Stayed a spell with a few of his friends and then rode out."

"You happen to know where he might have gone?"

"No, sir," the bartender said, "I do not. And I know better than to ask. What people do and where they go is their own business. You look like the kind of man that ought to know that."

Shiloh ignored the mild rebuke. "Well, I'm just anxious to find him," he said, tossing down his whiskey and heading for the next saloon in hopes that its bartender would be a little more informative.

Bill Hays poured himself a glass right next to Shiloh's and raised it in toast. "To friendships," he said. "To you and Dawson, to me, and to everyone that pays for a drink."

Shiloh nodded, clinked his glass against Bill's and said in a voice too low to be overheard by anyone else, "You have any idea where my friend and his boys might have gone?"

Hays studied Shiloh carefully and then said, "You're one of his gang, aren't you? And you need to be in on

BLOOD BOUNTY

whatever Dawson is planning."

"You got that plumb right," Shiloh said. "I'm about as broke as an old plow horse."

"You could get an honest job right here in town."

"Yeah?"

"That's right. I could use a little help myself."

"Doin' what?"

"Emptying spitoons, cleaning glassware, hauling liquor in and out, collecting money from the customers that suddenly decide they don't want to pay for what they just drank."

"No thanks."

Hays frowned. "Why not? I'd pay you . . . oh, a couple of dollars a day. It'd be enough to keep body and soul together until your friend and his boys show up again."

Shiloh sighed heavily. "Well, you see, Bill, the truth of the matter is that I'm just too set in my ways to do hard, honest work."

"You're an outlaw, is that it?"

"I prefer to be called a highwayman," Shiloh said, sounding a little offended.

"You probably even roll drunks for their pocket change, don't you."

Hays's friendly air was gone now and Shiloh could see the real man he faced, and what he saw he did not much like. Bill Hays wasn't really very nice at all.

"I don't rob drunks as a matter of course," Shiloh said. "I'd rather rob a bank, a train or a stagecoach. Now why don't we stop playing games and you just tell me where Harry Dawson went."

"All right. If you won't do honest work for honest pay, then I guess you might as well go join up with Harry."

Shiloh waited while the man rubbed a glass and then finally looked up and said, "I'm pretty sure that Harry is camped up in White Rock Canyon."

"Where is that?"

"About thirty miles away. Over near Elk. You musta heard of it."

"Heard of it? Hell, I just rode over from there!"

Hays shrugged. "Sounds like you came a long ways out of your way for nothing. Anyhow, that's the rumor—White Rock Canyon."

"You want to give me a little more specific directions?"

"Go back to Elk. They'll be able to tell you how to get to that canyon."

"Thanks," Shiloh said, turning and walking toward the door.

"Hey!"

Shiloh turned, and Bill Hays raised a bottle in a mocking toast as he crowed, "Don't you roll any of *my* drunks while you're here."

Shiloh's hand flashed down to the gun on his hip, and when it came up he fired. The bottle of whiskey exploded in the bartender's fist and pieces of glass lacerated the man's hand and arm.

"Hey, gawdamn you!" Hays shrieked. "I'll have you shot for that!"

Shiloh ignored the hollow threat and the astonished looks on the other patrons' faces as he went outside, belched and then headed for the livery. It had been a long, hard day of riding and he needed a good night's sleep.

He was angry for coming so far in search of Dawson only to discover that the man wasn't even in town. But that was the way it went hunting men—sometimes you felt like a dog chasing its own tail, going around and around in circles and getting nothing or nowhere.

But Dawson was close. Shiloh could feel it in the marrow of his bones, and he was bound to find the outlaw and his gang sooner than later.

20

SHILOH LEFT PINE City before daylight the next morning. He was stiff and in an ill humor. To make matters worse, a sudden rain squall drenched him to the skin and his teeth chattered for three hours before the sun broke through the clouds and warmed his bones.

His intention was to return to Elk, and once there he would get a little food and rest before getting directions to wherever the hell this White Rock Canyon was located. If he just got Harry Dawson in his rifle sights for an instant, he would wound the man bad enough that he could not escape but would not die.

Shiloh was dog tired and his horse was almost staggering when he rode back into Elk. If he'd kind of hoped for a warm welcome as a returning hero, he was sorely disappointed because people hardly acted as if he were alive. When Shiloh arrived back at old Walt Hostettler's livery, he stiffly dismounted and said to the man, "It's amazin' how a man can be a hero one day and scarcely worth a nod of a fella's head the next."

"What are you talking about?" Walt asked.

"Just that when I left everyone couldn't thank me enough for killin' Cephas. I ride back today and they look at me like I was a stranger."

"*You* killed Cephas?"

"Well sure! Who else?"

"Mike Harding. He's told the story of how he killed

Cephas to everyone who'll listen."

"Mike said *he* killed Cephas?"

"Well, didn't he?"

"Hell no! I'm the one that shot that old varmint, though I gave him a fair chance to defend himself."

Walt scratched his head and pulled up his bib overalls. "Well, sir, according to Mike, you were upstairs in Cephas's bedroom when the shooting began."

"Well I'll be damned!" Shiloh swore. "I don't believe this! So what has Mike been doing since I've been riding my ass off trying to nail down Harry Dawson?"

"Not much except swillin' free whiskey and suckin' up all the adoration."

"Has he been training that big blue stallion to race?"

"Hell, the stallion hasn't been out of its stall since it arrived."

Shiloh ground his teeth together and seethed with anger. "I reckon it's time that boy and I had a good talk. It would seem that he is in danger of having fame plumb ruining him."

"He's taken to it like a duck to water, all right. He used to be right shy and modest. Not anymore. You should hear him talk!"

"I don't think that would be good for his health," Shiloh said, handing his reins over to Walt and heading for the door. "Where is he? The Blue Dog?"

"Yep. Probably with a whiskey in one hand and a woman in the other."

"We'll fix that!" Shiloh groused as he headed up the street.

Returning to the Blue Dog Saloon, he found Mike Harding sitting cross-eyed drunk in a chair with a whore in his lap. When Mike saw Shiloh he blinked and tried to push the woman off of him, but she hugged his neck and after a few minutes of feeble struggles, he gave up and gave Shiloh a weak grin.

Shiloh did not grin back. He reached out and grabbed the woman by the arm and hauled her to her feet.

"Hey!" she cried. "Let go of me!"

"Take off," Shiloh said roughly, "me and the hero here are in need of a little private conversation."

Mike paled. He started to wobble to his feet but Shiloh pushed him back down in his chair.

"Now before you get riled," Mike said, "I'd like to explain!"

"Explain?" Shiloh snatched a fistful of Mike's shirt and hauled him to his feet. "Why don't your tell these folks who really had to do most of the gun work at the Circle Bar and who was upstairs hiding behind the bedroom curtains!"

"Well, you were!"

"I was *where*?"

"Downstairs. You're the one that gunned down Cephas and everything!"

Shiloh pushed Mike back down in his chair. He turned to the saloon's patrons. "It ain't that I'm proud to have killed any man, it's just that it galls the hell out of me to see a man crowing over what he didn't do."

The men nodded and turned away.

"Aw," Mike said, "I didn't mean any harm. You've probably had lots of folks look up to you like a hero. I was just enjoyin' myself."

"You've enjoyed yourself long enough," Shiloh said. "You were supposed to be training Diablo for us, remember?"

"Yeah, but—"

"Do it! Starting first light tomorrow morning."

"But—"

"I'll be there at the livery and you'd better be there too," Shiloh said, turning away in disgust and moving to the bar. "Whiskey on the house!"

"Yes, sir, Mr. Shiloh!"

Early next morning found Mike Harding sober and working hard as he saddled the blue roan stallion. Mike was still hobbling a little from the horse's bite on his leg and he was very careful not to allow the animal to inflict any more pain.

"I figure," Shiloh said, saddling his own horse, "that we can ride a little ways out of town and then race back in."

"Race?"

"Why sure! I know my poor horse is no match for yours, but—"

Mike interrupted by saying, "Walt has a sorrel Thoroughbred stallion out back that he brags can outrun anything he ever saw. Maybe you could get him to race it against us. Won't do the stallion any good if he hasn't got a challenge."

Shiloh frowned. He could see Mike's point. When the stallion shot out ahead and immediately began to run away from his own horse, it wouldn't really be a race at all.

"I'll ask Walt if we can race the mustang stallion against the Thoroughbred," Shiloh said, heading for the little room inside the barn that Walt used as his sleeping quarters.

When Shiloh awakened the old liveryman, Walt was not a bit pleased with the idea. "That Thoroughbred stallion belongs to Horace Utley, a rich man that's passin' through. It'd be up to him if he wants to race you or not."

Shiloh frowned. He hadn't really been thinking in

BLOOD BOUNTY   157

terms of a race, not this early at least. But if there was competition that would arouse heavy betting, this might be too good an opportunity to be missed.

"Where can I find this Mr. Utley?"

"He's stayin' at the Outland Hotel."

"First, I think I'd better take a look at the Thoroughbred."

Shiloh considered himself a pretty good judge of horseflesh and he saw at once that the Thoroughbred was a fine animal. It was as tall as Diablo, but not quite as muscular. "You seen it run, Walt?"

The liveryman shook his head. "Nope. But I got a hunch it's damn fast. Utley has done a heap of bragging and I'm betting that horse is where he's made most of his money these past few years. Do you really think that blue killer mustang of yours can beat a horse like this?"

"I've seen a few Thoroughbreds run before," Shiloh said. "But none of them could match Diablo. Besides, we'll just stretch the race out a little longer. That mustang stallion is tougher than boot leather. He can run all day and never get winded."

"Utley won't agree to a race beyond what this Thoroughbred can run fast."

"I'll talk to the man right now," Shiloh said as he left for the hotel.

He found Horace Utley in the hotel lobby reading a paper. The man was dressed in a suit, white shirt and starched collar and he wore a gold watch and chain that would have set a man back a hundred dollars.

Shiloh introduced himself but Utley made it clear by his frown that he considered Shiloh his inferior. "You say you have a mustang stallion you want to race against my horse? Ha! Mister, you don't look like you could raise two bits if your life depended upon it!"

"I'll raise you a hundred dollars and give you even odds," Shiloh said hotly.

"Oh, really?" Utley stood up. He was short, heavyset, and smelled of French cologne. "Well, then, in that case, let's have ourselves a horse race. When and where?"

"This afternoon, let's say, at five o'clock," Shiloh said, "and we'll race around town."

"This afternoon is too early. I need some time to find a good rider and then—"

"This afternoon," Shiloh said, pushing the man. "Or not at all."

Utley glared at him. "How many times around Elk?"

"Five."

"That's absurd!"

"Then four."

"Way too long."

"All right. Three and that's my bottom. Three times around won't be much more than a mile."

"Three it is," Horace Utley said, grinning. "But before I race, I'll want to see your money."

"You will," Shiloh promised.

Utley chuckled. "A mustang! Ha! That's rich. What is this critter's name?"

"Diablo," Shiloh said between gritted teeth. "And frankly, mister, he'll make your fancy Thoroughbred look like a plow horse."

Utley found that enormously funny and he was still laughing as Shiloh stomped out of the hotel, wondering where he was going to find the one hundred dollars stakes money he'd need to put up for the horse race.

He went tromping back to Walt Hostettler. The old man was notorious for being stingy and Shiloh had a feeling that he'd have a pretty good stash of money hidden away.

"Hell no!" Walt swore. "I don't think that your mustang stallion can run with a Thoroughbred!"

"He can!" Shiloh insisted.

"That's right," Mike said. "Trust us, Walt. You know that I know horses."

"You're a hell of a bronc buster, all right," Walt conceded. "But you don't know Thoroughbreds. And that sorrel stallion was bred to run."

"So was Diablo. Listen, if we lose your money, we'll make it up. I swear we will."

"With what?"

Mike looked at Shiloh, who said, "Hell, Walt. I'll double your losses with the bounty I get from bringing in Harry Dawson."

Walt shook his head. "All right," he said finally. "Your words?"

"Our words," Mike and Shiloh said in unison.

"I'll get the money," Walk grumbled. "But only because I don't like that rich son of a bitch Utley. Nothing would please me more than to see him and his fancy horse lose to a common old American mustang."

Shiloh grinned and clapped his young friend on the shoulder. "We'll do it!" he crowed. "We'll come out of this with a satchel full of money."

"Yeah," Mike said. "We're going to get rich quick."

21

BY LATE AFTERNOON, word had gotten out to the surrounding ranches about the high-stakes horse race, and there were more than a hundred people in Elk. Shiloh realized that he was nervous, and it didn't help when he saw that Horace Utley had hired one of the best riders in western Wyoming, Pete Mumford, to ride his Thoroughbred. Mumford was small and wiry and was an experienced race rider. The betting was heavily in favor of the Thoroughbred.

"I've faced up to shoot-outs and not been this jittery," Shiloh admitted to Mike as race time neared and they saddled Diablo. "Are there any rules that need to be followed?"

"Didn't you set any terms with Mr. Utley?"

"No," Shiloh said. "I guess the winner is just going to be whoever crosses the finish line first."

"Yeah," Mike said, nervously. "I just hope this son of a bitch behaves long enough to win."

"He will," Shiloh said. "He's *got* to or we're going to wind up giving everything we own to Walt. Diablo is a two-to-one underdog. If he wins, we ought to walk away with a sack full of money. I begged and borrowed every dollar I could lay my hands on and bet it on the mustang."

"He'll win," Mike said. "I never seen a horse that could run so fast."

"I saw Mumford warming up that Thoroughbred and he looks damned fast."

Mike snorted with false bravado. "He'll eat Diablo's dust the first time around and then he won't even be close enough to do that."

"That's the spirit," Shiloh said, already feeling better about the outcome.

When the two fine stallions came to the starting line, the crowd grew hushed. Shiloh cupped his hands to his mouth and shouted, "Three times around the town and the first one to cross this same line is the winner. Does everyone understand that?"

The crowd murmured with excitement. Diablo's eyes were flashing and he was raising hell, dancing, snorting, kicking and trying to get at the crowd and its horses. The Thoroughbred, on the other hand, looked calm and collected. Pete Mumford was composed and looked very confident. Shiloh drew his pistol and raised it overhead.

Beside him, Horace Utley made a few last-minute bets and hissed, "Before you fire that pistol, there's a matter of a hundred dollars that you need to put up."

"It's in my pocket," Shiloh said as he began to squeeze the trigger of his Colt.

"Ready! Set!"

The gun exploded in his fist and the Thoroughbred was off first. It flashed past the line of spectators, devouring ground with huge strides. Mumford was leaning forward so that his head was practically in the sorrel's flaxen mane. The crowd cheered for the favorite and it took what seemed like forever for Mike to get Diablo to line up in the right direction and then bolt off after the sorrel.

"A mustang!" Utley chortled, rocking back and forth with mirth. "A mustang! I'm almost ashamed to take your poor money."

"Don't worry, you won't have to."

"I'm even willing to take a side bet—even money—that my horse laps your horse."

"How much?"

"Name it."

"Another hundred?"

"Fine," Utley said, "and mister, you'd better have the money."

"Don't worry," Shiloh grated, "I always pay my bets."

Shiloh wanted to kill the arrogant bastard but he didn't. Instead, he watched as Mike finally got Diablo to run, but the mustang stallion wasn't running particularly straight or fast. Instead, it was dodging from side to side at the spectators, teeth flashing, ears flat against its head. It was all that Mike could do to keep the stallion from smashing into the crowd.

"That's a killer!" Utley said in anger. "He can't run and he's a menace!"

"He's a menace, all right," Shiloh said, "but he can also run."

When Diablo finally got past the spectators and out in the open, he did run. His tail lifted like a banner and he began to stretch out as he disappeared from view. Still, Shiloh knew that the blue mustang was a good quarter mile or more behind the Thoroughbred, and this was confirmed several minutes later when the racehorse with Pete Mumford on its back swept into view and then came thundering past the starting point. The crowd cheered the heavy favorite, and Mumford felt so confident that he raised one hand in a salute.

Seconds ticked by and then Diablo appeared running strong, but when he saw the big crowd up ahead, he hesitated. His eyes rolled and he snorted but Mike Harding was able to keep him racing forward. He was a blue flash as he shot past the crowd, and everyone who saw him gaped in amazement at the speed at which he was running.

"He's hopelessly behind," Utley said, jamming a cigar between his teeth. "That Thoroughbred of mine has never been beaten once he's gotten a fair-sized lead."

"There's a first time for everything," Shiloh said as Mike and the mustang disappeared at the far end of town on their second loop around Elk.

When the Thoroughbred came streaking past again, it was covered with sweat and running hard and was definitely winded. You could hear its labored breathing and it seemed to have lost a little speed.

"It's farther than I thought around this two-bit town," Utley commented, smoking rapidly.

"Diablo is closing," Shiloh said, "and he hasn't even broken into a sweat."

The next two minutes were tense as the townspeople waited for the Thoroughbred to appear again. When it finally did, they started to cheer but the cheer died prematurely when they saw Diablo moving up on the flagging sorrel like a wicked bird of prey.

And then, only a few hundred yards from where Shiloh waited at the finish line, it happened. Diablo overtook the sorrel in a rush and bit it on the rump. The Thoroughbred squealed in pain, lost stride and tried to kick. Mike could be heard shouting but not nearly as loud as Pete Mumford, who was trying to whip Diablo across the muzzle and drive the mustang off.

"What's that horse doing?" Utley cried. "He's . . . he's trying to kill my horse!"

Shiloh couldn't argue the point, especially when Diablo suddenly clamped his massive jaws on the Thoroughbred's neck and tore a chunk of flesh loose. Then he bit Mumford on the thigh, and the rider screeched and bailed off the sorrel. Mumford hit the dirt and bounced wildly into the crowd as Diablo shot past the sorrel and finished the race a winner.

"Foul! Foul!" Horace Utley cried over and over. "That mustang fouled my horse!"

Shiloh saw Mike struggling to keep Diablo from going after a man that had jumped out in his path with a whip. It was chaos, and Diablo plunged into the crowd, teeth snapping. Someone drew a six-gun and started shooting as the crowd dove for cover. When Shiloh saw the roan stallion again, it was vanishing into the distance with Mike riding low on its back.

Shiloh was mobbed and nearly beaten to death by the crowd. He had to draw his gun and hold them at bay until he could get the betted money that he'd managed to cover away from the man entrusted with holding the stakes. Someone punched him in the jaw and he almost went down, but he managed to stagger over to his waiting horse.

Utley was cursing like a man gone wild and the townspeople were rioting. It was all that Shiloh could do simply to spur his horse out of Elk in the direction Mike and the mustang had taken.

Son of a bitch! Was that any way to win a horse race!

Shiloh thought not, but his coat pockets were stuffed with greenbacks and, after all, Elk owed him a considerable favor. One thing for certain—after this, neither he nor Mike were going to be considered local heroes.

22

MIKE RODE IN the lead, rifle in fist, body stiff and alert as they slowly picked their way up through the rocky hills toward White Rock Canyon. They had been moving steadily through the moonlight for almost four hours and Shiloh judged that it would be light in just a short while.

Suddenly, Mike raised his rifle to the sky and reined Diablo to a standstill. He twisted around in the saddle and whispered, "White Rock Canyon is just up ahead, I think."

"You think?" Shiloh's voice took on an edge of warning. "You've got to do more than just think. You've got to be sure."

"Well, I can't be. I've never approached from the side before. This wasn't my idea, you know."

"Quit crabbing and keep riding," Shiloh ordered. "How high are the walls of the canyon, anyway?"

"Seventy or eighty feet."

"Then don't ride over the edge," Shiloh warned.

"Not on this horse, I won't."

Shiloh knew what Mike meant. He was riding a mustang and there was no better animal for picking its way up a dark, dangerous trail. A horse like Utley's Thoroughbred would have broken its leg or walked off the trail many times causing a wreck, but not Diablo.

Every time Shiloh thought about yesterday's fiasco in

Elk, he had to grin. Holy cow! What a race! Diablo was going to make them a fortune before it was all said and done. Oh, sure, he needed a good deal of discipline and training in manners, but speed and endurance were the things that won horse races.

"Pssst!"

"What now?"

"We're there," Mike said. "I can see the canyon."

Shiloh dismounted and tied his horse far out of reach of the big blue son of a bitch. He made a wide berth around the stallion on foot and came to the lip of the canyon.

"You sure this is the one?"

"Damn sure." Mike sniffled. "What do we do now?"

"I say we look for a way down real quick so that we can be among them at the break of dawn."

Mike gulped. "Maybe I ought to stay up here and watch the horses."

"You do what you think is best," Shiloh said, trying to hide his disappointment. "I'm not going to railroad anyone into a fight. But together, the chances are a lot better that we can take them all by surprise without a shot being fired."

Shiloh started moving along the canyon's edge. It wasn't a steep drop and he was able to find a game trail that would take him to the canyon floor.

"You comin'?"

"I'm thinking on it," Mike said after a long pause. "But if I go, you've got to give me your word I'll get half the reward."

"If you're in on this, you'll get half. If you stay up here, you get nothing. Which is it going to be, dammit? The sun is about to break over the eastern hills."

"But we don't even know yet if they're down there!"

BLOOD BOUNTY

"I can smell the smoke from a campfire," Shiloh said. "They're down there all right. Now come on!"

Mike followed him but with such reluctance that Shiloh wasn't at all sure the young bronc buster would be any help.

They made a rapid descent, and just as the first gray light broke over the eastern lip of White Rock Canyon, Shiloh saw the Dawson gang's horses. Rifle in hand and gun ready on hip, Shiloh moved quickly through the horses and found the camp. In an instant, he judged that there were only six sleeping men. Even so, when he twisted around to see Mike, the young rider was as pale as the dying stars.

Shiloh went over to Mike and leaned close. "Use your rifle to smack them across the head good and hard."

Mike recoiled. "You mean knock them in the head while they're sleeping!"

"Why sure! That way we can tie 'em up and get them on their horses before they can even think about giving us any problems."

"I don't know if I can do that," Mike hissed.

Shiloh grabbed the man's arm. "Dammit, you've got to do it. These are killers."

Mike nodded and Shiloh headed for the nearest man. He walked right over to the man, measured the distance and whacked him hard with the barrel of his rifle. The sound of steel striking flesh was a familiar one to Shiloh, but not to Mike, who took a retreating step as the man on the ground grunted with pain, twitched and then went limp.

"Come on, Mike!" Shiloh whispered frantically as he moved swiftly over to another one of the outlaws and clubbed him hard.

"Hey, what the . . ."

Shiloh spun a quarter turn to see one of the men sit up in his blankets. "Get him, Mike!"

Mike was frozen, but when the man on the ground reached for a gun at his side, Mike jumped forward swinging his rifle and it connected solidly across the side of the outlaw's head.

The last three outlaws came awake instantly, and one of them managed to grab his weapon and fire. But the man was groggy and the light was poor. Shiloh dropped to one knee and winged the man, who dropped his gun and shouted, "Don't shoot!"

Shiloh expelled a deep breath and squinted into the poor light. "Which one of you is Harry Dawson?"

There was a murmur of confusion. Finally, one of the men stammered, "Mister, ain't none of us are Dawson!"

"What?"

"Harry Dawson and his gang was all shot a couple days ago on the Comstock Lode trying to pull off a bank robbery!"

"No!"

"Yes, sir!"

"Then exactly what in the hell are you boys doing out here?"

When none of them answered, Mike happened to look at the campfire and he exclaimed, "Look, Shiloh! It's a running iron."

Shiloh saw the iron. He turned back to the men. "You're cattle rustlers?"

"No, sir!" one of the men cried. "Well, not exactly. We're just collecting abandoned cattle."

"What the hell is that supposed to mean?" Shiloh demanded.

When none of them volunteered an answer, Shiloh levered another shell into the Winchester. "I'll give you to the count of three and then I'll start shooting. One. Two."

"They're Circle Bar cattle!" one of the men cried. "Mr. Cephas Beck is dead and everybody is grabbin' what they can! We found these cattle, drove 'em up here into this canyon thinkin' that no one would find us, then you come along and . . . hell, mister! You can have 'em."

"Damn!" Shiloh swore. "I don't want those cattle."

"You don't?"

"Uh-uh," Shiloh grunted. "Mike, you want them?"

"Nope."

Shiloh did not lower his rifle. He was filled with disgust. "Let's get out of here!" he ordered, glancing back at Mike, who nodded with complete agreement.

"Hey!" one of the men shouted. "What about this bullet in my arm?"

"Find a doctor," Shiloh yelled as they hurried back up the game trail to the top of the canyon.

When they reached it, they were both completely out of breath and Shiloh was furious.

"I can't believe that Harry Dawson and his gang was so stupid as to get themselves shot before I could capture them and get that big reward!"

"It must happen now and then," Mike said, not sounding one bit disappointed in the morning's outcome. "Besides, we still have all that money we won in Elk. Why don't you just give up the bounty huntin' business and let's see if we can't train Diablo to race."

"That stallion will never stop trying to take a bite out of folks," Shiloh groused, still upset at the way things had turned out with Dawson.

"Yeah, but I've been studying on that problem," Mike said as he moved toward Diablo, sidestepped flashing teeth and vaulted into the saddle. "What would you think about getting a good saddlemaker to fashion us a muzzle?"

"A muzzle?"

"Yeah," Mike said, "and perhaps even insert a metal pot in it before he rigs a headstall."

"Diablo would hate it."

"He hates everything anyway."

"Good point," Shiloh conceded.

"Besides," Mike was saying as he reined the stallion about and headed off along their back trail, "Diablo would only have to wear it when we raced him."

Shiloh rolled a cigarette as he rode along. "It'd look damn strange, a blue racehorse wearing a cooking pot on his snout."

"That's right," Mike said over his shoulder, "but at least we wouldn't have to fight our way out of every damn town that we raced him in."

"That's true."

"Yes, sir," Mike said, sounding cheerful for the first time since Shiloh had met the man, "I think you, me and this killer stud I'm ridin' are going to be long remembered after our racing days are over and we are rich and retired!"

The thought was pleasant and Shiloh chuckled at the vision of Diablo streaking across a hundred finish lines with a pot hanging on his big, ugly blue face.

It would just serve the ornery son of a bitch right.

SPECIAL PREVIEW!

Introducing John Fury. Gunfighter. Legend.
Where there's trouble, there's . . .

FURY

Silent but deadly, he has no history and no home.
His only desire is justice.

Following is a special excerpt from this riveting new Western series—available from Berkley books . . .

FURY KNEW SOMETHING was wrong long before he saw the wagon train spread out, unmoving, across the plains in front of him.

From miles away, he had noticed the cloud of dust kicked up by the hooves of the mules and oxen pulling the wagons. Then he had seen that tan-colored pall stop and gradually be blown away by the ceaseless prairie wind.

It was the middle of the afternoon, much too early for a wagon train to be stopping for the day. Now, as Fury topped a small, grass-covered ridge and saw the motionless wagons about half a mile away, he wondered just what kind of damn fool was in charge of the train.

Stopping out in the open without even forming into a circle was like issuing an invitation to the Sioux, the Cheyenne, or the Pawnee. War parties roamed these plains all the time just looking for a situation as tempting as this one.

Fury reined in, leaned forward in his saddle, and thought about it. Nothing said he had to go help those pilgrims. They might not even want his help.

But from the looks of things, they needed his help, whether they wanted it or not.

He heeled the rangy lineback dun into a trot toward the wagons. As he approached, he saw figures scurrying back and forth around the canvas-topped vehicles. Looked sort of like an anthill after someone stomped it.

Fury pulled the dun to a stop about twenty feet from the lead wagon. Near it a man was stretched out on the ground with so many men and women gathered around him that Fury could only catch a glimpse of him through the crowd. When some of the men turned to look at him, Fury said, "Howdy. Thought it looked like you were having trouble."

"Damn right, mister," one of the pilgrims snapped. "And if you're of a mind to give us more, I'd advise against it."

Fury crossed his hands on the saddlehorn and shifted in the saddle, easing his tired muscles. "I'm not looking to cause trouble for anybody," he said mildly.

He supposed he might appear a little threatening to a bunch of immigrants who until now had never been any farther west than the Mississippi. Several days had passed since his face had known the touch of the razor, and his rough-hewn features could be a little intimidating even without the beard stubble. Besides that, he was well armed with a Colt's Third Model Dragoon pistol holstered on his right hip, a bowie knife sheathed on his left, and a Sharps carbine in the saddleboot under his right thigh. And he had the look of a man who knew how to use all three weapons.

A husky, broad-shouldered six-footer, John Fury's height was apparent even on horseback. He wore a broad-brimmed, flat-crowned black hat, a blue work shirt, and fringed buckskin pants that were tucked into high-topped black boots. As he swung down from the saddle, a man's voice, husky with strain, called out, "Who's that? Who are you?"

The crowd parted, and Fury got a better look at the

figure on the ground. It was obvious that he was the one who had spoken. There was blood on the man's face, and from the twisted look of him as he lay on the ground, he was busted up badly inside.

Fury let the dun's reins trail on the ground, confident that the horse wouldn't go anywhere. He walked over to the injured man and crouched beside him. "Name's John Fury," he said.

The man's breath hissed between his teeth, whether in pain or surprise Fury couldn't have said. "Fury? I heard of you."

Fury just nodded. Quite a few people reacted that way when they heard his name.

"I'm . . . Leander Crofton. Wagonmaster of . . . this here train."

The man struggled to speak. He appeared to be in his fifties and had a short, grizzled beard and the leathery skin of a man who had spent nearly his whole life outdoors. His pale blue eyes were narrowed in a permanent squint.

"What happened to you?" Fury asked.

"It was a terrible accident—" began one of the men standing nearby, but he fell silent when Fury cast a hard glance at him. Fury had asked Crofton, and that was who he looked toward for the answer.

Crofton smiled a little, even though it cost him an effort. "Pulled a damn fool stunt," he said. "Horse nearly stepped on a rattler, and I let it rear up and get away from me. Never figured the critter'd spook so easy." The wagonmaster paused to draw a breath. The air rattled in his throat and chest. "Tossed me off and stomped all over me. Not the first time I been stepped on by a horse, but then a couple of the oxen pullin' the lead wagon got me, too, 'fore the driver could get 'em stopped."

"God forgive me, I . . . I am so sorry." The words came in a tortured voice from a small man with dark curly hair and a beard. He was looking down at Crofton with lines of misery etched onto his face.

"Wasn't your fault, Leo," Crofton said. "Just . . . bad luck."

Fury had seen men before who had been trampled by horses. Crofton was in a bad way, and Fury could tell by the look in the man's eyes that Crofton was well aware of it. The wagonmaster's chances were pretty slim.

"Mind if I look you over?" Fury asked. Maybe he could do something to make Crofton's passing a little easier, anyway.

One of the other men spoke before Crofton had a chance to answer. "Are you a doctor, sir?" he asked.

Fury glanced up at him, saw a slender, middle-aged man with iron-gray hair. "No, but I've patched up quite a few hurt men in my time."

"Well, I am a doctor," the gray-haired man said. "And I'd appreciate it if you wouldn't try to move or examine Mr. Crofton. I've already done that, and I've given him some laudanum to ease the pain."

Fury nodded. He had been about to suggest a shot of whiskey, but the laudanum would probably work better.

Crofton's voice was already slower and more drowsy from the drug as he said, "Fury . . ."

"Right here."

"I got to be sure about something . . . You said your name was . . . John Fury."

"That's right."

"The same John Fury who . . . rode with Fremont and Kit Carson?"

"I know them," Fury said simply.

"And had a run-in with Cougar Johnson in Santa Fe?"

"Yes."

"Traded slugs with Hemp Collier in San Antone last year?"

"He started the fight, didn't give me much choice but to finish it."

"Thought so." Crofton's hand lifted and clutched weakly at Fury's sleeve. "You got to . . . make me a promise."

Fury didn't like the sound of that. Promises made to dying men usually led to a hell of a lot of trouble.

Crofton went on, "You got to give me . . . your word . . . that you'll take these folks through . . . to where they're goin'."

"I'm no wagonmaster," Fury said.

"You know the frontier," Crofton insisted. Anger gave him strength, made him rally enough to lift his head from the ground and glare at Fury. "You can get 'em through. I know you can."

"Don't excite him," warned the gray-haired doctor.

"Why the hell not?" Fury snapped, glancing up at the physician. He noticed now that the man had his arm around the shoulders of a pretty red-headed girl in her teens, probably his daughter. He went on, "What harm's it going to do?"

The girl exclaimed, "Oh! How can you be so . . . so callous?"

Crofton said, "Fury's just bein' practical, Carrie. He knows we got to . . . got to hash this out now. Only chance we'll get." He looked at Fury again. "I can't make you promise, but it . . . it'd sure set my mind at ease while I'm passin' over if I knew you'd take care of these folks."

Fury sighed. It was rare for him to promise anything to anybody. Giving your word was a quick way of getting in over your head in somebody else's problems. But Crofton was dying, and even though they had never crossed paths before, Fury recognized in the old man a fellow Westerner.

"All right," he said.

A little shudder ran through Crofton's battered body, and he rested his head back against the grassy ground. "Thanks," he said, the word gusting out of him along with a ragged breath.

"Where are you headed?" Fury figured the immigrants could tell him, but he wanted to hear the destination from Crofton.

"Colorado Territory ... Folks figure to start 'em a town ... somewhere on the South Platte. Won't be hard for you to find ... a good place."

No, it wouldn't, Fury thought. No wagon train journey could be called easy, but at least this one wouldn't have to deal with crossing mountains, just prairie.

Prairie filled with savages and outlaws, that is.

A grim smile plucked at Fury's mouth as that thought crossed his mind. "Anything else you need to tell me?" he asked Crofton.

The wagonmaster shook his head and let his eyelids slide closed. "Nope. Figger I'll rest a spell now. We can talk again later."

"Sure," Fury said softly, knowing that in all likelihood, Leander Crofton would never wake up from this rest.

Less than a minute later, Crofton coughed suddenly, a wracking sound. His head twisted to the side, and blood welled for a few seconds from the corner of his mouth. Fury heard some of the women in the crowd cry out and turn away, and he suspected some of the men did, too.

"Well, that's all," he said, straightening easily from his kneeling position beside Crofton's body. He looked at the doctor. The red-headed teenager had her face pressed to the front of her father's shirt and her shoulders were shaking with sobs. She wasn't the only one crying, and even the ones who were dry-eyed still looked plenty grim.

"We'll have a funeral service as soon as a grave is dug," said the doctor. "Then I suppose we'll be moving on. You should know, Mr. . . . Fury, was it? You should know that none of us will hold you to that promise you made to Mr. Crofton."

Fury shrugged. "Didn't ask if you intended to or not. I'm the one who made the promise. Reckon I'll keep it."

He saw surprise on some of the faces watching him. All of these travelers had probably figured him for some sort of drifter. Well, that was fair enough. Drifting was what he did best.

But that didn't mean he was a man who ignored promises. He had given his word, and there was no way he could back out now.

He met the startled stare of the doctor and went on, "Who's the captain here? You?"

"No, I . . . You see, we hadn't gotten around to electing a captain yet. We only left Independence a couple of weeks ago, and we were all happy with the leadership of Mr. Crofton. We didn't see the need to select a captain."

Crofton should have insisted on it, Fury thought with a grimace. You never could tell when trouble would pop up. Crofton's body lying on the ground was grisly proof of that.

Fury looked around at the crowd. From the number of people standing there, he figured most of the wagons in the train were at least represented in this gathering. Lifting his voice, he said, "You all heard what Crofton asked me to do. I gave him my word I'd take over this wagon train and get it on through to Colorado Territory. Anybody got any objection to that?"

His gaze moved over the faces of the men and women who were standing and looking silently back at him. The silence was awkward and heavy. No one was objecting, but Fury could tell they weren't too happy with this unexpected turn of events.

Well, he thought, when he had rolled out of his soogans that morning, he hadn't expected to be in charge of a wagon train full of strangers before the day was over.

The gray-haired doctor was the first one to find his voice. "We can't speak for everyone on the train, Mr. Fury," he said. "But I don't know you, sir, and I have some reservations about turning over the welfare of my daughter and myself to a total stranger."

Several others in the crowd nodded in agreement with the sentiment expressed by the physician.

"Crofton knew me."

"He knew you have a reputation as some sort of gunman!"

Fury took a deep breath and wished to hell he had come along after Crofton was already dead. Then he wouldn't be saddled with a pledge to take care of these people.

"I'm not wanted by the law," he said. "That's more than a lot of men out here on the frontier can say, especially those who have been here for as long as I have. Like I said, I'm not looking to cause trouble. I was riding along and minding my own business when

I came across you people. There's too many of you for me to fight. You want to start out toward Colorado on your own, I can't stop you. But you're going to have to learn a hell of a lot in a hurry."

"What do you mean by that?"

Fury smiled grimly. "For one thing, if you stop spread out like this, you're making a target of yourselves for every Indian in these parts who wants a few fresh scalps for his lodge." He looked pointedly at the long red hair of the doctor's daughter. Carrie—that was what Crofton had called her, Fury remembered.

Her father paled a little, and another man said, "I didn't think there was any Indians this far east." Other murmurs of concern came from the crowd.

Fury knew he had gotten through to them. But before any of them had a chance to say that he should honor his promise to Crofton and take over, the sound of hoofbeats made him turn quickly.

A man was riding hard toward the wagon train from the west, leaning over the neck of his horse and urging it on to greater speed. The brim of his hat was blown back by the wind of his passage, and Fury saw anxious, dark brown features underneath it. The newcomer galloped up to the crowd gathered next to the lead wagon, hauled his lathered mount to a halt, and dropped lithely from the saddle. His eyes went wide with shock when he saw Crofton's body on the ground, and then his gaze flicked to Fury.

"You son of a bitch!" he howled.

And his hand darted toward the gun holstered on his hip.

If you enjoyed this book, subscribe now and get...

TWO FREE

A $7.00 VALUE—

If you would like to read more of the very best, most exciting, adventurous, action-packed Westerns being published today, you'll want to subscribe to True Value's Western Home Subscription Service.

Each month the editors of True Value will select the 6 very best Westerns from America's leading publishers for special readers like you. You'll be able to preview these new titles as soon as they are published, *FREE* for ten days with no obligation!

TWO FREE BOOKS

When you subscribe, we'll send you your first month's shipment of the newest and best 6 Westerns for you to preview. With your first shipment, two of these books will be yours as our introductory gift to you absolutely *FREE* (a $7.00 value), regardless of what you decide to do. If you like them, as much as we think you will, keep all six books but pay for just 4 at the low subscriber rate of just $2.75 each. If you decide to return them, keep 2 of the titles as our gift. No obligation.

Special Subscriber Savings

When you become a True Value subscriber you'll save money several ways. First, all regular monthly selections will be billed at the low subscriber price of just $2.75 each. That's at least a savings of $4.50 each month below the publishers price. Second, there is never any shipping, handling or other hidden charges—*Free home delivery*. What's more there is no minimum number of books you must buy, you may return any selection for full credit and you can cancel your subscription at any time. A TRUE VALUE!

A special offer for people who enjoy reading the best Westerns published today.

WESTERNS!

NO OBLIGATION

Mail the coupon below

To start your subscription and receive 2 FREE WESTERNS, fill out the coupon below and mail it today. We'll send your first shipment which includes 2 FREE BOOKS as soon as we receive it.

Mail To: **True Value Home Subscription Services, Inc. P.O. Box 5235
120 Brighton Road, Clifton, New Jersey 07015-5235**

YES! I want to start reviewing the very best Westerns being published today. Send me my first shipment of 6 Westerns for me to preview FREE for 10 days. If I decide to keep them, I'll pay for just 4 of the books at the low subscriber price of $2.75 each; a total $11.00 (a $21.00 value). Then each month I'll receive the 6 newest and best Westerns to preview Free for 10 days. If I'm not satisfied I may return them within 10 days and owe nothing. Otherwise I'll be billed at the special low subscriber rate of $2.75 each; a total of $16.50 (at least a $21.00 value) and save $4.50 off the publishers price. There are never any shipping, handling or other hidden charges. I understand I am under no obligation to purchase any number of books and I can cancel my subscription at any time, no questions asked. In any case the 2 FREE books are mine to keep.

Name

Street Address   Apt. No.

City   State   Zip Code

Telephone

Signature
(if under 18 parent or guardian must sign)   744

Terms and prices subject to change. Orders subject
to acceptance by True Value Home Subscription
Services, Inc.

Classic Westerns from
GILES TIPPETTE

Justa Williams is a bold young Texan who doesn't usually set out looking for trouble...but somehow he always seems to find it.

__BAD NEWS   0-515-10104-4/$3.95

Justa Williams finds himself trapped in Bandera, a tough town with an unusual notion of justice. Justa's accused of a brutal murder that he didn't commit. So his two fearsome brothers have to come in and bring their own brand of justice.

__CROSS FIRE   0-515-10391-8/$3.95

A herd of illegally transported Mexican cattle is headed toward the Half-Moon ranch—and with it, the likelihood of deadly Mexican tick fever. The whole county is endangered... and it looks like it's up to Justa to take action.

__JAILBREAK   0-515-10595-3/$3.95

Justa gets a telegram saying there's squatters camped on the Half-Moon ranch, near the Mexican border. Justa's brother, Norris, gets in a whole heap of trouble when he decides to investigate. But he winds up in a Monterrey jail for punching a Mexican police captain, and Justa's got to figure out a way to buy his brother's freedom.

For Visa, MasterCard and American Express orders ($10 minimum) call: **1-800-631-8571**

FOR MAIL ORDERS: CHECK BOOK(S). FILL OUT COUPON. SEND TO:	POSTAGE AND HANDLING: $1.50 for one book, 50¢ for each additional. Do not exceed $4.50.
BERKLEY PUBLISHING GROUP 390 Murray Hill Pkwy., Dept. B East Rutherford, NJ 07073	**BOOK TOTAL** $ ____
NAME_____	**POSTAGE & HANDLING** $ ____
ADDRESS_____	**APPLICABLE SALES TAX** $ ____ (CA, NJ, NY, PA)
CITY_____	**TOTAL AMOUNT DUE** $ ____
STATE_____ ZIP_____	**PAYABLE IN US FUNDS.** (No cash orders accepted.)
PLEASE ALLOW 6 WEEKS FOR DELIVERY. PRICES ARE SUBJECT TO CHANGE WITHOUT NOTICE.	350